SAVIOR
BOOK I

KING HEROD

SAVIOR
BOOK I

KING HEROD

Amyzonn Knight

HEROIC ENTERTAINMENT INC.

EPIC ENTERTAINMENT TIMLESS FAITH

Edited by Shekhinah Byfield 2016

Copyright © 2016 Text Amyzonn S. Knight/Heroic Entertainment Inc.

Reg. No. 1134443

ISBN 13:978-0995842908

Copyright © 2016 Cover Illustration Amyzonn S. Knight/Heroic Entertainment Inc.

Copyright © 2016 Map by Yuliya Yanishevska

Stock Images provided by Shutterstock.com

Published by Heroic Entertainment Inc. Established 2008

DEDICATIONS

To my Lord and Savior

Jesus Christ

&

In Loving Memory of my mom

Merline

The SAVIOR BOOK SERIES is

Based on the Heroic Entertainment Inc.

SAVIOR PLAYS

Written, Directed & Produced by

AMYZONN KNIGHT

Inspired by the Events recorded in the Holy Bible

and the Historical Journals of Josephus

CONTENTS

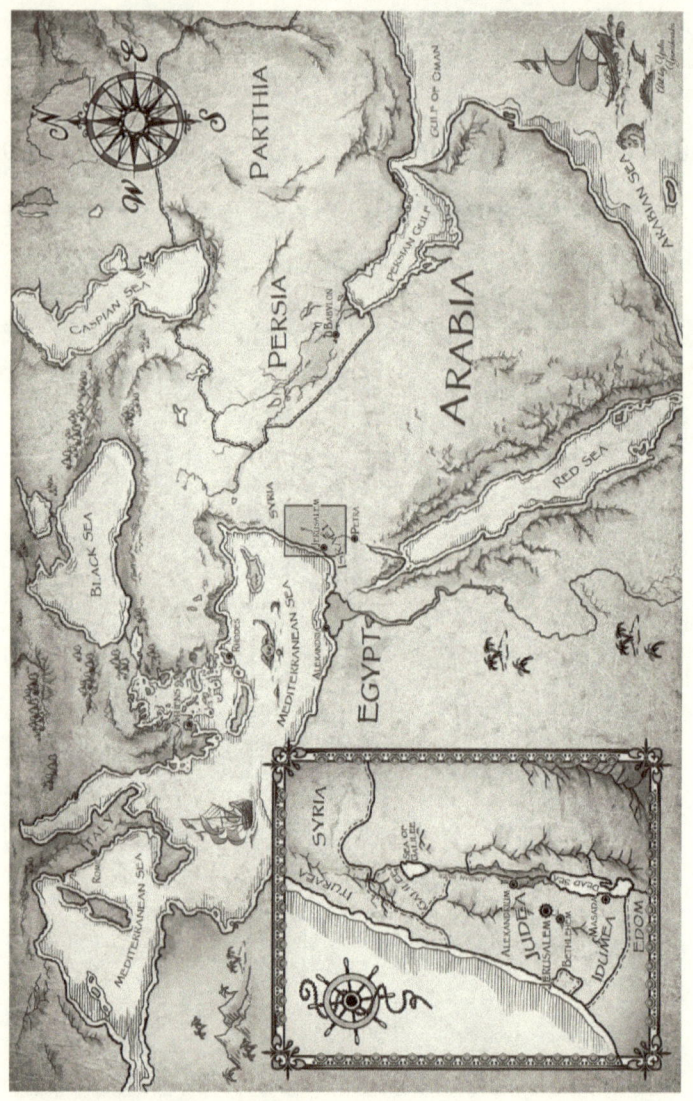

MAP OF HEROD'S TRAVELS

PRELUDE

Their screams echoed throughout the heavens as they fell, blazing a fiery trail through the cold blackness of space; plummeting like stars towards the blue planet at unfathomable speeds. Insurmountable in numbers, they rained down upon the earth—blazing fireballs turning the sky crimson and choking the atmosphere with streams of black smoke. Slamming into land and sea, one after another, their descent leveled mountains, turned boulders into dust and decimated the landscapes. Yet, none had the impact of what followed.

The sky turned black, exploding with violent winds, followed by a ground-shaking rumble of thunder. Suddenly, a fireball ripped through the atmosphere striking the earth like a bolt of lightning, hitting with catastrophic force. The impact sent earthquakes rippling in all directions from a massive crater that boiled the sea and plunged the earth into utter darkness. Silence ensued.

For a long time, nothing moved except a steady stream of ash, falling to the ground. The earth was dark and desolate. Then slowly, signs of life began to emerge across the landscape. Skin charred, feathers burnt, wings broken or severed, one by one they emerged: that great army destined to rule Heaven—or so they had been led to believe by the one who crawled up out of the massive crater. Covered in soot and ashes, shrouded in smoke, steam rising from his seared skin, his majestic crown replaced with a pair of horns, he stood up. His bloodshot eyes filled with rage, he looked up to Heaven and roared like a savage beast.

Bearing witness to the dawn of Creation and realizing they were imprisoned on earth, a general named Beliath approached the great fallen angel and asked, "What now, Prince Lucifer?"

Seething, the Devil looked on mankind and growled, "Vengeance!"

With one lie, he caused mankind's downfall, now our only hope rests in the promise of a Savior— a Man who will crush the enemy and redeem us from the grasp of hell.

For 4,000 years, we have watched for signs of His arrival; while the evil ones lurk in the shadows waiting to do one thing...stop Him.

1

THE PROMISE

[Around 100 B.C.]

A thick layer of smoke blanketing the landscape obscured all but the outlines of the tents. The camp, previously occupied by the wives and children of King Jannaeus' army, was now eerily silent. Two scouts, named Eshed and Gadish, climbed down off their horses. With sword in hand, they quietly made their way through the camp. The ground and tents were splattered with blood, yet there were no bodies in sight, not so much as a trace. "Where are our people?" Eshed whispered. "Did the Egyptians take them hostage?"

"Eshed, look at this," Gadish called, pointing to a large caldron resting on smoldering flames. The men approached it cautiously looking around. Steam was rising from the massive bubbling pot, and the air was laced with a disturbingly fowl aroma, one they were not familiar with. The men looked at one another and peered inside. Gadish asked, "Who made soup?" Eshed shrugged, but just as they were about to move on, he spotted something bobbing up and down, just beneath the surface. "Gadish, what is that?" He pushed his sword into the water and dug around. His sword emerged with the tip pushed through the eye socket of a human skull. Realizing what it was, he dropped it. Startled, the two of them peered into the caldron and stirred the water. To their horror, they saw boiled body parts and bones surfacing. The pot was filled with them. Aghast, they looked around; there were similar caldrons scattered throughout the camp, each one filled with bones and body parts.

As they realized why everyone had disappeared, looking around, Eshed dropped his weapon and fell to his knees, wailing, "My wife! My children!!" Gadish held him as he anguished. The fate that had befallen their Judean kin had become horrifyingly apparent—Prince Ptolemy and his Egyptian army were cannibals!

****

It was early morning. The day was warm and beautiful, not a cloud visible in the sky. Despite the news of the Egyptian prince's tirade on Judea, life in the capital seemed unaffected. The sound of birds chirping and children playing echoed throughout the streets of Jerusalem, while the smell of fresh bread and various meats sizzling over open flames, filled the air with a pleasant aroma.

Merchants were busy, gathering in narrow alleys and large squares beneath colorful canopies, setting up their stalls, whilst the beggars and the lame made their way into the streets to lay claim on their favorite spots—where they expected the crowds to be thickest. Dozens of women were gathered by the riverbanks washing clothes, dying fabrics and chattering among themselves, whilst out in the countryside, farmers were loading up their carts with grain and produce to bring into town, and herdsmen were driving their flocks and herds out to graze.

Feeling a sudden chill in the air, a shepherd, napping on a wide branch of a tree at the top of a hill, sat up. His sheep that were grazing, started bleating. Dark storm clouds were rippling across the sky, and hearing a rumble below, the shepherd looked down. Beneath the gathering clouds, he saw a vast army in the valley riding toward Jerusalem, and behind them was an unseen army of demons driving them forward with rage.

In Jerusalem, a servant sweeping the temple courtyard shooed off some children playing outside the gate. He chuckled to himself as he watched them run off and then continued sweeping. The air suddenly thickened and filled with an icy chill that could only be felt by the most discerning of spirits. The servant stopped and looked up. For a moment, the air smelt fowl, like sulfur, stinging his eyes and nostrils. A sudden crack of thunder echoed across the sky, followed by a loud thud emanating from the shadows of the temple. The servant took a few timid steps towards it, but when he saw a large crack travelling up the temple wall and along the ground towards him, he dropped his broom and ran off.

Under the guise of the storm, a creature had arrived in the realm of men, landing in the temple with a heavy thud. A howling gust of wind snatched at the jagged tail of his black robe and ruffled the feathers of his large black wings. Invisible to man's eyes, a massive fallen angel stood up and emerged from a cloud of dust. His face, though still bearing remnants of his former beauty, was gnarled. The ridges of his brow protruded up and outwards. His eyes were like two black pearls staring out from beneath an iron helmet crowned with jagged horns. Beliath—now known as *Destroyer*, the lord of Destruction—stepped out from the darkness, having opened a doorway from the Dark Realm.

The demon towered like a titan between the marble pillars of the temple as he peered out, surveying the landscape. Busy streets were lined with thousands of sandstone buildings. Tens of thousands of people going about their daily lives were oblivious to the evil that had ascended, or the decimation they intended to bring. To the demon-lord, man appeared as images through the haze on a hot day. They were small, feeble creatures, insignificant to him and the powerful army that waited in the shadows, waiting to destroy...every living thing. Invisible to man, they wouldn't even see them coming, not until it was too late.

His army had been divided in two. Half were driving the Egyptians towards the gates of Jerusalem, and the other half remained veiled in the darkness, ready to step through the portal at the demon-lord's command. Equipped with heavy armor, he wore a breastplate bearing the crest of a 3-headed serpent, large spiked shoulder guards, (each larger than a man's head) and heavy iron greaves and manicas. With a pair of swords harnessed between his shoulder blades and a long curved one on his hip; a large shield bearing the same crest as his breastplate, boarded by an intricate design of the ailing faces of the most powerful men he had slaughtered, the demon-lord looked over the landscape then commanded, "Come forth!"

Beneath the veil of a dark, turbulent sky and rumbling thunder, demons stepped from the realm of darkness into the realm of man. Tens of thousands more were waiting to come through. All shapes and sizes, some clad with armor and weapons, others bearing hideous horns and grotesque protrusions, they gathered while *Destroyer* bellowed, "Our brothers drive the bloodthirsty Egyptians towards the gates! And from within, we shall strike the city with fear, terror and chaos! Until Jerusalem's streets run red with blood amidst a pile of rubble! We shall see what becomes of the promise of man's Savior, when his people are wiped from the face of the earth!" His words were met by the rumble of demons cheering beneath the stirring of a violent wind.

The colossal lord of Destruction drew his long, curved sword. He raised it high and roared, "DEATH TO ALL!!" They lunged forward, only to be halted by a blinding flash of light, striking the temple entrance with a ground-shaking thud.

The demons shielded their eyes as three huge figures stepped out through a dispersing waft of smoke—angels. Their white garments and golden armor, glistened. The largest of the three—an archangel, stepped forward. His impressive white wings, gleaming like sunlight through the clouds, spanned beyond the width of the temple entrance. Beneath a golden breastplate, his white robe—trimmed with gold—glimmered, and his decoratively designed golden greaves and manicas shone like polished glass.

On his head rested a magnificent helmet, rimmed with creeping vines culminating around the crest of a lion, and was crowned with rubies around a luminescent white horsetail. The helmet tapered down to a point between his brilliant golden eyes—they blazed like fires. He sported a finely trimmed beard, mustache and long, raven locks shimmering with golden highlights against his bronze skin. Chiseled jawline and muscular in form, he was a flawless image of rugged beauty and raw strength. Carrying a silver and gold shield in his left hand, the angel folded in his wings, stepped forward and spoke with a thunderous voice. "Beliath! Or should I say...*Destroyer!*" At the sound of his voice, fragments of the dark army began to retreat.

"Michael!" *Destroyer* scowled, standing his ground. "I should have known you would come."

"And yet, here you are, desecrating holy ground." Michael's golden eyes pierced the darkness like flashes of lightning. "It was not enough that you used King Jannaeus to turn Queen Cleopatra against her son—Ptolemy, just so you could unleash his wrath on Judea, but you also drove him to massacre women and children, and commit the most heinous of acts!"

"Yes, and it worked. He and his men now march on Jerusalem with an army of demons at their back, ready to slaughter every Judean in the kingdom!"

"...While the rest of your army clambers from the darkness to sow fear and terror from within. Is that your plan?"

"Something like that. Are you here to watch your precious city fall?"

"No..." Michael drew his massive sword and declared, "I am here to stop you."

Destroyer looked at the two angels behind the archangel, and clanking his sword against his shield, snarled, "Then you should have brought more!"

He charged at Michael, savagely attacking him, while the others watched. Michael fought back, locking up *Destroyer's* shield against his. "Your quest is futile. At this very moment, an Egyptian army rides to stop the rogue prince." He shoved the demon back.

"You're too late!" *Destroyer* raged before lunging at him again. He delivered several powerful strikes with his sword, which Michael met with equal force then turned the attack on him. *Destroyer* managed to block it, and then suddenly spreading his black wings, kicked the archangel in the chest, sending him reeling into the other angels. Michael stood up and glared at him. *Destroyer* smirked, and then with a glance, several large demons immediately ran in and attacked with massive axes and spears, serving as a distraction while *Destroyer* prepared an ambush, but the other angels jumped into the fight. *Destroyer* suddenly came running in, leaping at Michael, his sword over his head. Before he could strike, the archangel backhanded him with his shield, sending the demon-lord flying through the air. He landed with a heavy thud.

Enraged, *Destroyer* sprung up, threw down his shield and roared, "You think you can stop us! If I cannot kill them with the sword, then I will destroy them with earthquakes and plagues!!"

"Not today!" Michael responded.

Destroyer and the rest of the demons who had made it through the portal, charged at the angels, but all three dropped to one knee and lifting their swords, thrust them into the ground. The earth shook, splitting in three directions and hurling the demons back. A powerful blast of wind started to blow, throwing them back into the Dark Realm. Being the most powerful, *Destroyer* seemed resistant. While others were whipping past him, he dug his claws into the pillar, fighting with every ounce of his strength. Michael stood up, and unfolding his wings whilst peering at the demon-lord, declared, "Go tell your master...the Promise will *not* be broken! Man's Savior is coming! And there is nothing you can do to stop Him!" A powerful stream of fire blasted from Michael's eyes, burning into the demon's chest until it drove him through the portal, hurling him back into the Dark Realm. The archangel then used the fire from his eyes to seal the portal shut. Stepping out into the sunlight, he looked up into the turbulent sky, and in a flash of light, shot up into the clouds, while the other two angels disappeared. The clouds immediately began to disperse. The violent winds died down and the sky changed from gray to blue as a peaceful calm fell over the city, and all trace of the battle between angels and demons disappeared.

****

Being driven in blind rage by an invisible army of demons, as he entered a valley just outside Jerusalem, Prince Ptolemy found his path blocked by a vast Egyptian army. The prince raised his hand, bringing his army to an abrupt halt. His men were fierce, but when it came to numbers, they were no match to the full force of Queen Cleopatra's army.

Stationed in the chariot at the head of the queen's army was an Egyptian general named Helkias. Standing on either side of him, veiled from the eyes of men, were the two angels who had fought beside Michael. They watched as the general called out, "Prince Ptolemy! By order of the Queen, you are to cease your attack on Jerusalem and return to Egypt!"

"And if I do not?" the prince scowled.

The general lifted his hand. Immediately, five thousand archers with their bows in hand drew back their arrows and took aim at the prince's army.

"You dare threaten me, your prince!" Ptolemy raged.

With the demon army growing restless, the angels drew their swords and stepped forward. In an instant, they were at the back of Ptolemy's army, facing the demons. One of the angels named Xavier—Resembling a Cherokee Indian with a reddish-brown hue and long straight black hair—announced, "It's over! Now turn back!"

"Or what?" growled a large hideous demon standing over 12' tall. He stomped towards them carrying a spiked club the size of a man. "Who is going to stop us?" he asked, "You?"

The other angel named Jesiah—dark in complexion—pointed to the hills and replied, "No, them."

A vast army of angels appeared across the horizon. Their gleaming white garments and their golden armor glistened so brightly it blinded the demons. Each was stationed in a chariot of fire with their weapons trained on the demon army. "Jerusalem is protected!" Xavier shouted. "And your commander has been driven back into the darkness. Leave! Now! While you can!"

Looking up at the angelic army, several times their size, the demons descended into the ground, leaving Prince Ptolemy and his army to face the wrath of his mother. "Rome has threatened war on Egypt if you attack Jerusalem!" the general announced sternly. "With respect, my Prince, my orders are to stop you...by any means necessary."

With the demons gone and their rage now replaced by fear, Prince Ptolemy signaled his army to retreat under the watchful eyes of both Helkias and the angels before they too disappeared behind a veil of clouds.

****

In the Dark Realm, seated on a throne atop of a long staircase, a pair of yellow eyes peered out from beneath the shadow of a dark hood and stared down at *Destroyer* as he knelt before the throne. "My Prince..."

"Spare me your excuses..." Lucifer scowled with a dragon's tone, "You failed me...yet again."

"Michael...he is too powerful. We cannot destroy the city while he guards it." *Destroyer* murmured keeping his eyes to the ground.

"Then we need another plan," Lucifer hissed.

"He said there is nothing we can do to stop the Promise, the One who will destroy us is coming."

Lucifer pondered for a moment. "If we cannot stop Him, then upon His arrival...we will destroy Him."

"How?" asked *Destroyer*.

Lucifer leaned forward, his face visible in a dim shaft of light, he grimaced, "We need a weapon."

2

DESTINY

[74B.C.]

Landing at the entrance of a Jerusalem market, *Destroyer* stood up. This time he was the size of an ordinary man. Instead of wings, he had a tattered grey hooded cloak. As he drew it over his head, he became visible to men, not as a demon, but as an older man. With salt and peppered hair, a bushy beard and eyes, cold and fierce, he looked around and then headed into the market, blending into the crowd. He brushed past a man named Dathan examining a papaya at a fruit stall situated just inside the entrance of the market. After smelling the fruit, he grunted, "Give me three of those. Your best ones."

The merchant handed him the three papaya. Dathan put two into a small soft leather bag he had slug across his chest, and moved off. Just as he was about to eat the other one, a man suddenly grabbed him and shoved him against the wall, "Dathan!" he snarled, "I want my money!   You promised you'd pay me back three weeks ago. I know you've been avoiding me! I want my money NOW!"

Being a large, gruff man, Dathan shoved him off and scowled, "You'll get your money, Mashen, when I have it! Now get lost!" He shoved Mashen into the fruit stall, knocking both him and it over as he grunted, "You bother me again, and see what you'll get!" He strutted off into the market, eating his papaya without a care in the world.

Also, entering the market was a young slave-girl named Lydia. She stopped momentarily to look up at the Roman insignia mounted on the archway—a blatant reminder that they were under Roman rule.

The day was hot, and like most others, the market was crowded with people bustling past one another amidst greedy merchants vying for their attention.

"Fresh fruit!

"Exotic spices, used by the queen of Egypt!"

"Salted meats! Fresh fish!"

"Wine from Babylon!"

The propositions went on and on with every merchant claiming to have the finest products and the best deals. Lydia found her senses overwhelmed by a myriad of interesting aromas and sounds as she strolled from one stall to another.

Coming from the other direction, a young thief was making his way through the market. He moved through the crowd, snatching anything he could get his hands on, from food to brass utensils, and money, pushing them into pockets sown into his garment. When he spotted one stall selling gold and silver trinkets, he meandered around it until the merchant looked away, then snatched a beaded necklace and ran. Realizing he had stolen from her, the merchant shouted, "Thief!! Stop him!"

A couple of passing guards gave chase, barreling through the crowd, almost knocking Lydia into a stall as she turned the corner, but she managed to dart out of the way until they rushed past.

Once the excitement was over, things settled and everyone went about their business.

Lydia turned her attention to an archway leading to a narrow street called, 'Silk Alley'. She glanced up at the colorful canopies and even more colorful garments hanging over walls and market stalls. "I have the finest silks from Egypt, Persia and Babylon. Garments fit for a queen!" one merchant exclaimed, showing her some of her selections.

While the merchant tended to other customers, and Lydia thumbed through the hanging fabrics imagining what they might look like on, she saw a woman speaking to a crowd. Intrigued, she strolled over and listened. "People of Jerusalem, our Savior, the Messiah, he is coming soon..."

Dathan, who happened to be among those listening, jeered, "Is he now?" Glancing up at a pair of Roman soldiers passing by on the road, on the hillside above them, he sneered, "Is he coming soon enough to save us from our enemies?" His remark stirred up the crowd.

The woman looked at him and snidely remarked, "Not soon enough to save you."

Mocking her, he heckled, "Ooh! Is that supposed to scare me? You old crow! What do you know!" Turning to the crowd, he jeered, "She's a woman, since when does God speak to women! Get back to your pots and pans!" he grumbled walking off as the crowd dispersed. Passing a, "Tending to your own house is what you ought to be doing! You listen to that old wench..." he shouted, looking back at her, "and she'll have you believing we're all gonna di..." His words were cut short as he turned the corner and felt a shape pain in his chest. He looked down seeing the blade of a long dagger thrust into his chest.

"Nobody steals from me!" Mashen snarled as he pulled the dagger out. "Keep the money." He pushed Dathan back and glancing around, took off.

Gasping, Dathan staggered back out, just long enough to look at the woman and the dispersing crowd staring at him as he toppled backwards into a well. The crowd looked at the women, but she turned her attention to the servant-girl and grabbed her hand. "You..." Startled, Lydia stared at her. The strange woman with deep mysterious grey eyes peered out from beneath a long green shawl; she seemed to look right into Lydia's soul. "...your mistress is going to bear a son tonight." she remarked.

"How do you know who my mistress is?"

"Is she not wife to General Antipater, chief advisor to the crowned prince?"

Lydia stared at her bewildered. "How do you know that? I've never seen you before. Are you a seer?"

"I am," she replied.

The old man in the grey cloak strolled over to a nearby stall, pretending to look at hanging statues and wind chimes, while he listened to the seer.

"How I know is of no importance, what matters is that the child she will bear will one day become king."

"That is not possible," Lydia retorted. "My master and his wife are but servants of the royal house. They are not even Jewish."

"Believe me when I tell you, that child is destined to become king."

"You expect me to tell my mistress..."

The seer suddenly grabbed her hand, warning, "If you are wise, you will tell your mistress nothing."

"Then why are you telling me this?"

"Because, I have seen a great darkness within him and..."

Hearing the wind chimes blowing, the seer stopped and peered over Lydia's shoulders. The old man was hiding around the corner, listening.

Lydia dragged her hand away. "How do I know any of this is true and not the ramblings of some madwoman?"

"You will know I speak the truth when you hear the child's name," she replied, turning her attention back to her.

"And what name is that?"

Glaring at her, the seer replied, "Herod."

Sensing something as the old man peered around the corner, the seer stepped past Lydia and stared at the corner, but *Destroyer* was gone, leaving only a chime swinging in the wind.

Lydia looked around. "What is it?"

"Darkness..." The seer took a few steps forward. Peering around, she murmured, "It's searching for something."

Frustrated and wondering what she was rambling on about, Lydia insisted, "but what about the child?"

Looking back at her, the seer warned, "He must not become king."

"Why?"

Staring off into the distance, she replied, "Because I have seen what he will do."

****

It was close to midnight. Only torches and candles lit the room. The flickering flames and sheer curtains, blowing gently in the wind, were casting eerie shadows that danced across the walls and large marble pillars. Lydia stepped out through a doorway draped with heavy green and yellow curtains. There were pillars on either side of the entrance and ailing screams emanating from within. She headed to a small round table to fetch some water, when she heard a baby cry and the midwife announce, "It's a boy!"

Lydia watched her master enter through the curtain, while *Destroyer* watched from behind a pillar in the shadows.

Lydia started to pour out some water into a small bronze basin while she listened to them speaking.

"Behold your son," Cypros said wearily, "What shall we name him?"

His father announced, "His name shall be…Herod."

Startled, Lydia gasped, spilling some of the water. She stood there pondering. The seer's words were true—the question was...what to do about it? Upon hearing her mistress call her name, Lydia quickly sopped up the spilled water and picked up the basin. She stood before the entrance for a moment, gathering her composure, and then entered through the curtains.

Lurking in the shadows, smiling to himself, *Destroyer* returned to the Dark Realm to where Lucifer was sat on his throne. His yellow eyes were staring into the darkness, his mind filled with thoughts of violence: glimpses of his sword slashing at angels—memories of a time long past. He was suddenly drawn back to the present by *Destroyer's* announcement, "My lord, I believe I may have found what you seek...a weapon."

3

DARK REALM

Existing on a plain, parallel to mankind's, the Dark Realm existed in perpetual darkness. There was no day or night; neither sunlight or moonlight shone on this plain. Its only source of light came from fire. Some burned in fortresses built within temples and mountains, where those of higher rank hailed themselves as gods. Some was conjured up by powerful spirits wielding magic. The rest emanated from the occasional bolt of lightning and cracks in the ground leading down to hell.

The sky was dark and gloomy, filled with storm clouds continually rumbling with thunder. The atmosphere was thick with smoke, and carried the stench of death and sulphur. Violent winds howled, being driven by demonic spirits whipping back and forth. The ground—dry and crackled, was devoid of life; yet, it teamed with movement.   Legions of fallen angels were preparing for war, while insurmountable hideous demonic creatures crept about in the shadows. Feeding on fear and evil, their snarls and growls were the eerie chants that continuously echoed in the darkness.   It was by God's mercy that man's eyes were shielded from this realm.

Pitched atop of a massive volcano-like mountain, *Destroyer* crossed a black bridge. Dozens of gargoyles were perched on teeth-like pedestals, guarding the path leading up to Lucifer's throne. The demon-lord stopped at the foot of the black steps leading up to a large dais. Visible to all, across the northern plains of the Dark Realm were six massive golden urns ablaze with fire. They shone like beacons around Lucifer's throne, while an eerie mist continually poured down the mountain.

Lucifer's giant throne was forged from onyx and gold in the shape of a giant dragon. It gradated upward from black to gold. The dragon's claws rested on the back of the throne while its wings encircled it on the left and right side. Its tail curved around the footrest which was made up of human skulls. A pair of black serpents with eyes made of precious gems tapered up towards his grandiose armrest: a pair of gold and black wings—a reminder of what he had lost, fueling his rage. They rested on a pair of human skulls—symbolic of his rule over mankind.

Lucifer's lips teased upward into a sinister smile, "A servant who would become a king?" he mused as *Destroyer* approached him.

"Not just a king... From what I gather, there is much darkness in him," he replied. Gazing up like a dog seeking his master's approval, *Destroyer* asked. "Is that not what you seek?"

Lucifer glanced down at his advisors who sat on thrones hewn out of the mountain on either side of him.

An advisor to his left, named Pyro, remarked, "We can use that to your advantage, my lord."

"We shall see." The Prince of Darkness leaned forward and ordered, "Summon the old ones."

At the blast of a huge ram's horn, a mist covering the bottomless pit beneath the bridge began to stir. An echo of roars emanating from the pit's murky depths answered the call. Rocks began to crumble; the sound of heavy footsteps shook the dark chamber as demonic spirits as old as time itself, began to scale the walls of the pit.

Through a plume of mist rising from the pit they emerged, and unlike the fallen angels, these were powerful spirits forged in the dark crevices of Lucifer's heart. These were the firstborns of sin in which evil found its manifestation.

The first to emerge was a large four-winged, pale dragon. Its large claws left deep depressions in the stone as it climbed up. He stepped on the dais and transformed into a statuesque man with hollow, black eyes and silvery white skin. One set of wings changed into an Emperor's toga and tunic; the other set became an elaborate black and gold robe—looped across his shoulder and draped over his left arm. An extravagant crown formed on his head and large rings adorned his fingers. He stood with his head held high and a cold, condescending sneer on his pale face, wreaking of arrogance.

The next to emerge was a giant of a creature so large she could not fit onto the dais. From the waist down, she had multiple octopus-like tentacles for limbs, using them to glide up onto the dais, but unable to fit, half her body dangled over the ledge resting on a mound of treasure. From the waist up, she had the body of an obese female, apart from four long tentacles for arms and smaller tentacles from her head down to her waist tightly clutching trinkets. Draped in gold, she was adorned with an elaborately bejeweled gold crown that fanned up and outward like a peacock's tail. Beads draped across the back over plated gold scales that covered each of the numerous tentacles on her head.

Equally impressive was the intricately designed golden armor inlaid with precious gems and an exquisite golden robe draped over her shoulders—the envy of any king. She wore gold crowns like bangles on her smaller tentacles, and sported them like rings on many of the suction cups of her larger appendages—relics, no doubt, of all the kings she had conquered. With one look from Lucifer, she began to shrink down, using her tentacles to shove as much treasure as she could into the folds of her skin and the crevices of her armor. It wasn't only treasure she was hoarding, but also fine garments and food, upon which she gorged without restraint. Lucifer smiled when he saw her.

The mist turned green as another enormous creature emerged. She circled the dais, rapidly slithering through the crevices and emerging atop of a colonnade that encircled the throne. Two pairs of large peridot eyes, amidst dozens of smaller ones, peered down on them. Luminous scales shimmered in the darkness. Coiling its way down one of the black pillars, a giant two-headed serpent emerged. From the waist down, she was all snake, but like the octopus, her upper body was that of two seductive females with serpentine heads—Siamese twins. Their skin was covered in shimmering, luminous green, leathery scales, running in an intricate dark and light pattern.

Their eyes were bright green with sharp, spear-like, black pupils down the centers. A pair of narrow, gold crowns that tapered to a point between their eyes, sat on their heads amidst hair that was made of dozens of small green serpents. They all moved in unison, like shoals of fish, following the direction of their eyes. The two-headed creature moved with the grace and fluidity of a sea serpent.

They eyed everyone, including Lucifer, with a scrutinizing glare, while the octopus—eyeing their crowns—tried to snatch them off their heads with two of her tentacles. The three began to hiss at one another, but the bickering was brought to an abrupt end when a giant, red tipped scorpion stinger slammed into the ground between them from which veins of black venomous poison began to branch outward. It was followed by the heavy thud of a massive demon landing on the dais. Part man, part scorpion, he lifted his tail and recoiled it into a curved position over his head.

His skin was red with plates of a black exoskeleton, like a scorpion, running down chest, back and tail. Spikes jutted out along the curvature of each plate. Being armed with menacingly large pincers, he was the most formidable of the four.

His face—bearing a hint of several small spiked protrusions—was shrouded beneath his black plated cowl and a pair of inward facing horns. From the dark shadow within, the demon peered out with narrow slit, malicious red eyes, slanting upwards.

His venom continued to spread until it came into contact with Lucifer's feet as he stepped down from his throne. At that moment, the venom fizzled out. Lucifer smiled and announced, "*Malice*! My old friend."

"I am no-one's friend," Malice snarled.

"Of course, you are not," Lucifer said with a cold smirk. "You are the poison that seeps into men's hearts and takes root in the seed of hatred, spreading like a disease."

He shifted his eyes to the pale man and remarked, "And Pride—you scoundrel! Look at how you wear arrogance like a fine perfume. Stubborn as an ass, you blind men to reason. No wonder they fall when you go before them." Proud of himself, *Pride* lifted his head even higher and smiled.

Lucifer strolled over to the twin-serpents, running his fingers through their serpentine hair as he looked from one to the other. "Envy, your eyes are a particularly exquisite shade of green today. Far more alluring than your sister's." He shifted a sneaky glance in the direction of her twin sister—Jealousy, then looking back at Envy, remarked, "You know...I do believe of the two...you are the prettier one." Envy grinned, until a hand suddenly slapped the grin off her face. Jealousy was glaring at her and hissing. Bearing her fangs, Envy hissed back and started clawing at her sister's face and hair while Lucifer stood back and watched with a grin. As the two-headed serpent reeled and writhed back and forth, scrapping viscously, Lucifer glanced at Destroyer and smirked, "Girl fights..." After a few moments, Lucifer shouted, "Enough!" As the two calmed down, he said aloud, "You two are so gullible! Slaves to your nature!" He stepped towards them and remarked, "Self control...is what you two lack. You...who were the first to rear your heads—desiring all that was not yours. If not for you, I would still be servant to God...but instead, I am ruler...of a mound of dirt." Smiling, he took hold of their faces, and peering into their eyes as they pursed their lips, he said with a cold grin, "I don't know whether I should kiss you..." His smile fading and his grip tightening, he snarled, "Or torment you!"

After glaring at them for a moment, seeing them wince with pain, Lucifer smiled and released them, turning his attention to the plump octopus-demon. "And my favorite...*Greed*." He glanced at *Envy and Jealousy*, smirking at the look of resentment in their eyes as *Greed* caressed his face with one of her tentacles. "You consume the whole world: the rich, the poor, the great and the small; the one thing all men know is greed. They will kill and betray for you; even sell their own children. You have wrought more treachery and death than all others combined."

"Am I not at the route of all evil?" she gloated in between stuffing her face.

Wiping away a slither of food from her chin and licking his finger, Lucifer replied with a smile,

"Indeed, you are. Consume away, my pretty, consume away."

Lucifer looked across at *Destroyer*. Gesturing to him, he remarked, "And let us not forget the lord of destruction and war, shedder of blood, maker of weapons, and captain of my armies—*Destroyer!*" He stepped back and addressed them, "Look at you all! Magnificent! You were with me from the beginning, desolating kingdoms, laying waste to nations!" All six bowed before him. "Now, we have the means to destroy the Promise and lay waste to the One who threatens our rule over mankind!" With thousands of demons watching from every crevice in the mountain and his words being relayed across his kingdom, the Dark Realm erupted in rousing cheers that went on for some time.

When the cheers died down, *Malice* looked up and asked, "How are we to destroy Him?"

Lucifer responded smugly, "You leave that to me. For now, you have a new assignment, his name...is Herod."

4

HEROD

After pondering the seer's prophecy for several days, wondering if she should say or do something, Lydia stood over the child's crib watching him as he slept. The seer's words were ringing in her head, over and over—this child will be a king. After adjusting his covers, she closed the curtain and went out. Finding her mistress, Cypros, seated on the terrace with Herod's elder brother—Phasael, Lydia approached her and hesitantly said, "My lady, there is something you should know about your son, Herod."

Cypros put down her cup on a table and looked at her. "What is it? Is he ill?"

"No, he's fine."

"Then what is it?"

Lydia looked at the little boy. Realizing that it wasn't something she wished to share in front of the child, Cypros leaned over and said gently to him, "Run along now Phasael, and go play with Hippicus and the other children."

After the boy left, Lydia stepped in a little closer and wringing her hands nervously, confided, "The day of Herod's birth, I met a seer in the market. She told me...he was destined to become king."

Cypros looked at her strangely. "A seer said my son would be king?" Cypros chuckled. "Why do you listen to those soothsayers? How much did she charge you?"

"Nothing. She did not ask for money."

Cypros shrugged it off. "Even so, soothsayers always say what they think you want to hear. Their predictions are worthless..."

"She predicted that your son would be born that night, and that you would name him Herod."

Cypros glared at her. It seemed Lydia had gotten her attention. "She called him by name?"

Lydia nodded. "Yes."

"What else did she say?" The servant-girl shifted her gaze to the window, watching the curtains and the leaves blowing in the gentle breeze, pondering if she should continue. "Lydia!"

Cypros insisted, "What else did she say?" Lydia turned her gaze back to her mistress.

After hearing all that the seer said about her son, Cypros loaded up the child and her maid, along with a pair of guards and headed to the market. Though she refused to believe any of it, she needed to hear for herself what this supposed seer really knew about her son's destiny.

****

Arriving near noon, Cypros—accompanied by Lydia and the guards—headed into the market. "I believe she has a tent through here," Lydia called, leading them through the crowd. Upon spotting the seer's small tent just as they entered Silk Alley, Lydia pointed her out. "That's her."

With child in hand and the guards clearing her path, Cypros pushed her way through a dispersing crowd until she came to the entrance of the open tent. "My handmaid tells me you know things about my son?"

Busy securing the corner of her tent with 10" long nails as thick as her thumb, the seer didn't bother to look up, but simply murmured, "Oh, and who might your son be?"

"His name is Herod."

The seer halted. She turned around and looked at the child sleeping quietly in his mother's arms. She shifted her gaze to Cypros, then stood up and started to approach. One of the guards drew his sword and stepped between them, glancing down at the hammer and nail in her hand. The seer put them down on a rickety old table in the middle of the tent, on which there was an amalgamation of bottles, herbs and oils. The guard then lowered his sword and stepped back.

"I wish to hear what you have to say about my son?" Cypros demanded.

The seer glared at her, then peering over her shoulder and catching a glimpse of Lydia, she turned back to her table and tightened the cork on one of the bottles, murmuring, "What is it you wish to know?"

"I think you know."

The seer turned back to her and looked at the guards, unwilling to speak before them. Cypros handed the child to Lydia. "Take him and wait for me in the carriage."

"But..."

"Do as I say. Now go."

"Yes mistress." Though reluctant, Lydia took the child and headed back to the cart along with one of the guards.

Convinced that he would not be able to hear their conversation over the sounds of the noisy market, Cypros ordered the remaining guard to wait outside and ensure that no-one entered the tent. She then had him pull down the flap as she followed the seer inside. "Now...what do you know of Herod's destiny?"

****

The return journey back was quiet: Cypros seemed preoccupied with her thoughts. When they arrived at the palace, she went and poured herself a drink while Lydia changed and put the child to sleep. When the baby finally settled down, she closed back the decorative curtains around his crib and joined Cypros in the main quarters. "He's asleep now, my lady," she said timidly, gazing down at the marble floor.

"Good," Cypros murmured, pouring out a second cup of wine.

"Did the seer tell you what you wanted to know?" Lydia asked.

Cypros looked at her and smiled. She strolled over to her with the two cups of wine. Handing one to Lydia, she replied, "Yes, she did."

Lydia looked at the cup and shook her head. "I am still on duty, my lady."

"I am sure my husband will not mind this once." Lydia stared at the cup until Cypros insisted, "I want to celebrate my son."

The handmaid hesitantly took the cup. "Thank you, my lady."

Cypros raised her cup and said, "To Herod...the future king." Lydia smiled and knocked cups with her. Though both put the cups to their lips, Cypros watched her, and then lowered her cup and moved off.

"But what of the other things she said...the terrible things?" Lydia asked.

Cypros shrugged. "We came to an understanding."

"An understanding?" Lydia asked, feeling a discomfort in her throat.

Cypros remarked, "The seer warned you not to tell me, didn't she? You should have listened to her." She turned around and with an icy smile, emptied her cup onto the floor.

Wide-eyed, Lydia gasped and looked at her cup. Feeling her airway suddenly constrict, she dropped her cup and clasped at her throat. Unable to speak, she stared at her mistress, her eyes begging the question *"Why?"*

With eyes, cold and callous, Cypros explained, "I suppose I should thank you. Until now, our only hope of gaining real power was through my husband's control over that spineless prince, influencing his decision while we increase our position of strength with his allies. I never dreamed we could see one of our sons on the throne as king. As for the rest..." Her smile fading, she put down the cup and murmured, "Well...that seer will never speak of it again...and neither will you." Her lips blue and her eyes bulging, there was a sudden thud as Lydia fell to the floor. Her gasps soon fell silent and her body stilled.

A sinister smile curled on Cypros' lips. Upon hearing the baby fuss, stepping over Lydia's lifeless body, she went to retrieve her son from his crib and carried him out to the terrace. Stepping outside into the cool breeze, she went and stood beside her husband—General Antipater. A man of a dark complexion with cold, steely eyes, dressed in bronze armor with a red sash looped over his right shoulder, he asked, "It is done?"

"Yes."

"And what of the other loose end?"

Cypros shifted her gaze towards the eastern market beyond the palace wall.

****

Lucifer—possessing a white haired old man in a dark hooded cloak, and *Destroyer*—disguised as the stranger in the tattered grey coat—pushed their way to the front of a small crowd of people gathered at the entrance of the seer's tent, gazing down at her lifeless body. Her eyes wide open; she lay in a pool of blood, with a nail head sticking out of her temple. She had been nailed to the ground.

****

Cypros kissed her son and replied, "Taken care of."

"Good," said Antipater. "Now we can proceed with our plans."

"And what about the prophecy?"

Antipater gently rubbed his hand over his son's head and assured her, "No prophecy will shape our son's destiny. We will."

5

30 YEARS OF WAR

[40 BC...]

37 years of age, his skin—golden brown with a thin beard and a head of thick loose curls blowing in the wind, General Herod was seated on a black stallion with his brothers, kinsmen and his friend Hippicus at his side. Tall, handsome and as charismatic as he was brave, he shouted at the great army before him, and all those on Jerusalem's wall, "People of Jerusalem! I offer you terms of peace! You know the rightful king of Judea is King Hyrcanus! His brother, Aristobolus II, is dead! His son Alexander is dead! And now his youngest son—the man who sits on the throne—stole it from his uncle! This is a man who holds woman and children hostage! Turn over the usurper! Restore your king! And Jerusalem will know peace once again!"

"Roman lovers!" Antigonus shouted from his chariot, "Go back to your Roman masters, you Half-Jew dogs!" Then he started a chant that the crowd quickly joined in. "Go home, Half-Jews! Go home, Half-Jews!"

Herod looked at his brother, Phasael, "So that is their answer...insults." He raised his sword and with a war cry, led an alliance of Romans and the king's army into battle. A skilled warrior, wielding his sword with expert precision; he cut down the enemy as they charged into the midst of the battle.

****

"30 years of war!" Mira grumbled, stumbling over rubble as she and Anna made their way through the deserted streets. "I was a barely 14 when it started. All this is because of the queen. She caused this civil war with her foolish decision to name Hyrcanus, both King and High Priest.

"It wasn't all her fault," Anna objected. "He refused to share power with his younger brother."

"Queen Salome had two sons: Hyrcanus and Aristobolus. Hyrcanus may have been the elder, but why not name one King and the other High Priest?"

"Hyrcanus was already High Priest."

"Then she should have named Aristobolus, King."

"You know she would not do that, not when he sided with the Sadducees, and both she and Hyrcanus supported the Pharisees..."

"Pharisees! Sadducees! Who cares! This was never about religious politics, it was about power!" Mira stated angrily. "One had it, the other wanted it. Now, look where it's gotten us...30 years later, we're still at war."

"Watch out!!" Anna pushed Mira back against the wall as hundreds of arrows sailed over. They hit everything in their path, maiming and killing dozens of people and animals, not to mention, tearing through stalls and setting some aflame, along with roofs, carts and canopies. The women stood back as dozens of soldiers fell off the wall. Those the arrows failed to slay were killed by the fall.

"You see!" Mira scowled as they started to move off. "How many men have died in this cursed war? If not for the greed of those two princes, your husband and my son would not be out there on that battlefield. They'd be home where they belong, or tending the fields..."

"But they are out there!" Anna retorted as a soldier ran past them. "Besides, King Hyrcanus did try to make peace with his brother."

"What, by giving his daughter in marriage to Prince Alexander? A fat lot of good that did," Mira grumbled, rolling her eyes. "That peace treaty lasted just long enough for the prince to sire two children and then we were back at war. I mean, really...that crown has gone back and forth between Hyrcanus and his brother so many times, half the time, I didn't know which one to call king. One week it's, *All Hail King Hyrcanus!* By the next it's, *All Hail King Aristobolus!*"

"Well, he's dead now, him and Alexander," Anna said, trying—to no avail—to put and end to her grumbling. "Hyrcanus is our king."

"He was our king, until that..." glancing around, she quietly murmured, "Swine of a nephew of his showed up and seized the throne! At least Prince Alexander was a decent, but Antigonus...he is just like his father...all he cares about is power! He cares nothing for the people!"

Anna glanced up at the palace. "Do you think it's true that he's holding Princess Alexandra and her children hostage in the palace."

Mira shrugged, "Who knows...she should have fled with King Hyrcanus."

"I heard she refused."

"Probably because there's a rumor that Herod may have been involved with her husband's death."

Anna peered up at the palace and uttered with concern, "I wonder if that's why she stayed. Maybe she thought her brother-in-law wouldn't harm them."

Mira glanced up at the palace and murmured, "Then she thought wrong."

****

Hearing shrills outside as another barrage of arrows hit some of the palace guards, Princess Alexandra peered out the window. She looked back at her daughter, Miriam, huddled against the wall holding her younger brother. "Can you see anything?" Miriam asked.

Alexandra shook her head. "I can't tell whose winning. I think father's men are."

"What will happen to us if they lose?" Miriam asked.

"I don't know." Worried, Princess Alexandra went and sat down between them.

"I'm scared," said young Prince Aris, holding his mother tightly.

"Don't be afraid. Father will rescue us." She looked at Miriam and, forcing a smile, squeezed her hand as she turned her eyes towards the window.

****

"Look at this!" Mira grumbled, stumbling over corpses. "All because of that prince's greed."

"Like it or not, Antigonus holds the city," Anna hissed in a hushed voice. "And these are his men surrounding us."

"Not for long," Mira muttered, watching the fierce battle through a crack in the wall.

"What do you mean?"

"Take a look…" she stepped aside to let Anna peer through the gap.

"Herod's men are breaking through?" Anna muttered.

****

Herod drove his forces forward with a fierce ferocity, matched only by his ambition. The battle had dragged on for months, with both sides suffering significant loss; but as it approached dusk, the tide of battle seemed to turn. Herod slashed through several men, driving a path through the enemy. His sights were set on Prince Antigonus who stood in the safety of his chariot, positioned not too far from the city gates, barking orders at his men. When Antigonus saw the allied troops cutting through his men like paper, and spotted Herod on a warpath heading straight for him, the prince headed back towards the city gate.

Herod pointed at the prince and yelled to his commander—a large brutish man named Sohemus, "Don't let him get away!!" Sohemus immediately led a small party towards the gates, trying to cut off the prince's path, while Hippicus—an expert archer—and his men, picked off several soldiers stationed on top of the wall near the gates, with carefully aimed arrows.

****

Anna was still peering through the crack in the wall, ignoring Mira's calls as she searched the battlefield for her any sign of her husband. Catching a flash of blue on one of the soldier's arms, she called, "I think I see him!"

"Anna! We have to go!"

"Wait! I...I just want to see him!"

Mira peered out through the hole. All she saw was a chaotic melee of clashing swords and men being slaughtered. "How can you expect to find him in this battle?"

"I tied a blue ribbon to his left arm."

"It's not safe here! We have to move, now!" Mira took Anna's hand and dragged her from the wall. As they tried to navigate their way around corpses and debris, the women narrowly escaped another barrage of arrows, followed by dozens of wounded and dead soldiers falling off the wall, directly into their path. It might as well have been boulders falling around them. "Come on! We have to find shelter," Mira called, as she took Anna's hand and ran back against the wall. Through a crack, they saw several catapults being pulled back, each loaded up with a giant boulder. "This is madness! If we stay here, we're going to die!"

****

The Romans released the catapults. Huge boulders came flying through the air. One was heading in their direction. "Look out!!" Mira grabbed Anna and pulled her down just as a boulder crashed into the wall less than half a mile away. It slammed into the wall, knocking out dozens of large stones and sending an avalanche of rocks and mortar crumbling on top of a dozen men, whilst several others jumped, only to be crushed or left with broken limbs. Multiple boulders hit. The women screamed and huddled down. When the bombardment had stopped and the dust settled, discovering they were still alive and unhurt, Mira grabbed Anna's hand and dragged her to her feet. "Come on! We have to get to safety!"

As they started to move off, Anna saw a young soldier lying on the ground a few feet away from them. He was injured. His mouth filled with blood, he clutched at his ribs with one hand, and reached out to her with the other. "We have to help him."

"No, we don't!" Mira grunted, grabbing her hand.

"Mira, he's just a boy." Anna pulled her hand away from her friend and started to climb over the rubble.

"Anna!" Mira called, furiously gesturing for her to come back. Anna glanced back at her, and shook her head. She reached out to the young soldier, when suddenly, a large rock fell and slammed directly on top of him. His blood splattered over her face and clothes. Startled, Anna stood there, staring at it. All she could see of the boy was his crushed arm and feet. Mira came and grabbed her arms, dragging her away.

****

While Herod hacked and slashed his way through the enemy troops, his younger brother Seth, found himself beset by a large brute, aptly named Gurowl. He stood over seven feet tall: heavyset, seeming as big and strong as a bear. He even looked and growled like one *(which was why he earned his name).* He ploughed through several Roman soldiers, before heading straight towards the young man, knowing exactly who he was.

Gurowl knocked Seth's sword from his hand and then cracked him twice across the jaw, dropping him to his knees. A young man in his mid-twenties, Seth managed to block him and hit the beast with his shield. The soldier staggered back a little, but while Seth tried to recover his sword, the brute rushed at him. He ripped the shield from his hand and flung him and it several feet. Seth landed hard. It knocked the wind out of him. By the time he started fumbling back to his feet, the large soldier was marching towards him, cutting down three allied soldiers in his path. Seth barely had time to grab a nearby shield, before

Gurowl started beating down on it with the edge of his sword.

Shards of wood flying, Seth lay beneath the shield in a foetal position, shuddering under the impact of each savage blow as the edge of the heavy iron sword split the shield. The next blow tore through the flesh of his forearm. Agonisingly, he cried out. Terrified, he looked up through the crack knowing he was about to die as Gurowl lifted his sword, determined to split both the shield and the boy in two. Suddenly, the tip of a sword pierced through the brute's sternum, bringing him to a halt. Looking down at the blood-soaked iron blade protruding from his chest, the sword slipped from Gurowl's hands. He shuddered as the blade was withdrawn from his chest and staggered around to see Seth's uncle—Joseph, standing behind him with the bloody sword in his hand.

Stunned by his resilience, Joseph lifted his sword once more, but before he could stab him again, Gurowl grabbed his hand, crushing it in his bearlike grip, and with the other hand, grabbed his throat and squeezed.

Joseph clawed at his hand, but couldn't break his grip. Seth, realizing his uncle was in trouble, scrambled to his feet and hit the brute in the back with his shield until it broke. Yet, despite the massive wound through his back and chest, he didn't flinch. If he was going down, he was going slow and taking one of them with him.

Without his sword, and seeing Joseph gasping for air, Seth looked around at the enemy and grappled a weapon away from one of them, managing to overpower and force him to turn it on himself. Once, he had the sword in hand, he turned back towards Gurowl. Just as he raised the sword, a dagger came flying from the left and struck the brute in the neck. As blood started to spew out, his grip loosened, his eyes glazed, and then he fell back, hitting the ground with a thud. In the distance, both men saw Herod, his hand still posed from the throw. He smiled and joked, "You trying to get yourself killed? The battle is not won yet." He turned and swiftly slaughtered three enemy soldiers before spotting Prince Antigonus abandoning the battlefield. The city's defense was down, the wall was breeched and King Hyrcanus' troops were starting to spill inside. The prince's troops were defeated. His only options now were to surrender or run. He chose the latter, as did many of his men. Once the remainder saw the prince leaving, they laid down their arms and opened the gates. Herod's men erupted into cheers.

Still huddled against the wall with her daughter and son, Princess Alexandra flinched as they heard a thud at the door. Prince Antigonus had left a pair of guards outside the door, as well as a battalion of soldiers throughout the palace. And although Alexandra had told her children otherwise, she had overheard the instructions her brother-in-law left the guards in the event that they lose the battle: kill her and her son, and take her daughter captive. If he failed to win the battle, marriage to Princess Miriam—the king's granddaughter—was his only way to secure a legitimate claim to the throne.

Alexandra peered out the window; they were too high up to climb down. In desperation, she searched the room with her eyes, looking for anything she could use as a weapon, but the prince had removed every sharp object the day he had taken them captive. The only things remotely useful were a pair of tall candleholders and a few wooden chairs. With each thud, panic ensued, not so much for herself, but for her young son, a boy barely 14. "Stay here!" she ordered Miriam, as she kissed her son and got up.

"Mother, what are you doing?"

"What I must." Alexandra picked up one of the 6' candleholders, holding it like a spear.

Deciding it might be better as a club, she turned the wide end up and waited beside the door, bracing herself. The king may have been gentle and mild, but she was quite the opposite. Miriam went and picked up a chair, and then came and stood on the other side of the entrance. "What are you doing?" Alexandra whispered loudly.

"Helping."

As the doors burst open, Alexandra swung at the first person to enter, as did Miriam. Hippicus was the first in, followed by Herod. Luckily, Hippicus spotted the weapon and darted back out of the way. Herod, on the other side, sword in hand, caught Miriam's chair mid-swing. "My lady. You are safe now." Miriam stared at him, and he at her, quite enchanted by her beauty, as was she, by the strong, handsome man who had come to her rescue.

"Alexandra!" The king called from behind them.

"FATHER!" Princess Alexandra dropped the candleholder and ran to the king, flinging her arms around him. Miriam let go of the chair, leaving it in Herod's hands as she and her brother ran to the king.

"God be praised! You're all safe!" King Hyrcanus breathed a big sigh of relief. "Did he harm you?"

"No," Alexandra replied as they started walking out, telling the king of their ordeal.

Herod and Hippicus walked behind them. Sensing him staring at her, Miriam glanced back. Herod seemed unable to take his eyes off her. When Hippicus noticed, he looked at Herod and laughed. "Old friend...what are you thinking now?"

Herod smiled and replied quietly, "In all the kingdoms I have visited, I have never seen such beauty."

"Which one?"

Herod realized he was referring to the young prince Aris, who was equally as handsome as his sister was beautiful. Herod looked at Hippicus and clapped him across the back of the head, laughing.

6

SMITTEN

Sacrificial fires blazed in the temple. The streets were filled with celebrations: people cheering, dancing and singing, drowning out the sobs of those mourning the dead. Those loyal to Antigonus and brazen enough to protest against the king on the day of his victory were arrested and hauled off to the dungeons, while the High Priest conducted a ceremony, officially declaring Hyrcanus *King of Judea*.

Outside on the battlefield, hundreds of people started scavenging the dead. From soldiers and thieves to merchants and the poor, all were rifling through their clothing for weapons, money and anything else of value, before others came to bury them. Among them were Mira and Anna, not scavenging, but they were among the many wives and mothers in search of their loved ones.

While many of the people gathered at the temple for the lengthy ceremony in which the priests sacrificed 1,000 bulls to the Lord, an army of workers and slaves started clearing a path through the streets leading to and around the palace. The strong piled the dead onto carts and hauled them away to be buried, and used hundreds of oxen to drag the larger stones to the wall—they would be needed to rebuild it. Once the large rocks were moved from a spot, smaller fragments were piled onto carts and hauled away while the old and more feeble came behind them with large rakes and brooms to clear away any remaining rubble to allow the king to lead an unobstructed parade through the city.

Things would have gone as planned, if not for a handful of protestors. They pushed their way to the front of the crowd lining the streets and began hurling insults at the king and the royal party as they passed by. Their leader, a man named Simon, stood on a rock and yelled, "Behold the puppet and his puppet-masters return!! A fool with no spine who only speaks the words of those Edomite scum who Rome has appointed to govern us!!" He spat at Herod as he and his brother, Phasael, drove by in their chariots. Herod's commander, Sohemus, didn't wait for a command; he and several of his men immediately gave chase. The protestors scattered. Sohemus focused on their leader, trampling his way through the crowd, as he and two others followed Simon down an alley.

The encroaching sunset made it easy for Simon to slip into the shadows between two houses and disappear. The men couldn't follow him on horseback, and although they could have searched for him on foot, for all Sohemus knew, this was just a ploy to draw them away from the king, leaving him and the governors unguarded. As much as he would have liked to ring Simon's neck, Sohemus ordered his men to turn back. "You're a dead man!" he growled, "You hear me! DEAD!" He left the alley, while Simon watched him from darkness.

Despite the minor disturbance, the triumphant parade ended at the palace with a prestigious celebration that could be heard all the way to the hills surrounding Jerusalem, where Antigonus and his overthrown army had fled. Suffering a crushing defeat, their numbers now decimated, and barely escaping with the clothes on his back and a day's worth of supplies, the prince halted his horse just long enough to look back at the palace. Seeing torches blazing against the cerulean sky and hearing songs and cheers being carried on the wind, taunted him. He turned his eyes towards the mountains, marking Judea's borders, and murmured under his breath, "This is far from over."

****

The protestor incident forgotten, Herod and Phasael sat up on the large dais along with the king. They sipped wine and feasted their eyes on the colorfully dressed dancers moving in unison, across the mosaic marble floor of the banquet hall. The king stood up and gave a rousing speech, thanking those who had brought about this great victory. "Today, 30 years of civil war has finally come to an end!" The rest of the king's speech seemed to fade into a blur, as Herod watched the butler—Itiel, escort Princess Miriam, into the large hall.

She entered wearing an elegant red silk dress with a gold embroidered vale draped over her right shoulder. Long, dark curls gently brushed over her shoulders as she walked, and her flawless skin glowed with a golden shimmer under the flickering flames of the palace torches. He found himself so intoxicated by her breathtaking beauty, not even the treasonous slurs, being shouted through the citadel gates was enough to draw his attention. It was only when Phasael stood up, that

Herod heard the king say, "We owe this victory to our sons and our brothers! Our Roman friends! And the man who led this campaign! A man with his father's wisdom and his mother's charm...lord Herod!"

Herod stood as the crowd erupted in cheers. He discretely searched around the room with his eyes until he spotted the princess, while the cheers faded into silence and the expectant crowd waited. With all eyes on him, Herod lifted his cup and said, "I was a child when this war began. Forced to leave my home and my friends..." He glanced at Hippicus—the son of a palace servant and a childhood friend—who had been forced to remain behind when King Hyrcanus and his subjects had first fled the palace. It had been many years before they were reunited.

Herod turned his attention back to the crowd and continued, "...At the time, I did not understand what we were fighting for, but after so many years of turmoil and bloodshed, I soon came to realize that this war was about one thing...PEACE! Peace under the rule of a good and noble king! Those of us who have lived through war and the tyranny of rule under Aristobolus II, know that it was all worth it! Because today we have restored peace to our kingdom!" He raised his cup and shouted, "To Judea! And her rightful king! Long may he reign!!" The crowd erupted in cheers again, and taking back stage to King Hyrcanus, Herod put down his cup and stepped down off the dais.

"Where are you going, Brother?" Phasael asked in a jovial tone.

With a slight hesitation, Herod replied, "To greet our guests."

****

As Herod made his way around the room, the High Priest and one of the king's cousins—Rabbi Babas—watched him. Babas quietly remarked, "Speaking of Aristobolus...are you aware he was poisoned?"

The High Priest looked at him, startled, "No, I was not."

"Right in his own camp," Babas explained, sipping on his wine. "Rumor has it, the deed was committed by a spy. And guess who she worked for?"

"Who?"

Babas turned his gaze toward Cypros as she greeted the guests. Smiling at her, he muttered from behind his cup, "That conniving witch. She and her late husband have had the king wrapped around their little fingers for decades. No wonder the people call him a puppet."

The High Priest smiled at Cypros then turning around uttered, astounded, "The king would never agree to the murder of his brother?"

"Perhaps, he did not have a choice in the matter," Babas replied with a discrete glance around the room, ensuring they were not being overheard. "After all, people are saying the real power lies with Herod and his brother."

The two of them nodded and smiled at Herod as he glanced in their direction. Herod nodded and greeted them with an equally pretentious smile, before turning his attention to his cousin, Malchus, the King of Arabia. "So, tell me cousin...how many times did they stab Julius Caesar?" asked King Malchus, He was a distant relative of Herod's father—Antipater, and had lent his support to King Hyrcanus' campaign.

"23 times," Herod replied. On his way to find the princess, he had somehow become side-tracked by his cousin and a few inquisitive guests, and lost sight of her altogether.

"Ouch!" Hippicus muttered, joining them as he slushed back a cup of wine. "That must have hurt."

"He died on the Senate floor," Herod informed them in a sober tone. "It seems all those who opposed him, plunged a knife into him, sharing the guilt."

The stout Arabian king in colorful apparel, who loved to eat at every opportunity, plucked the largest leg of lamb off a platter as one of the servants passed by.

"Some have accused your father of aiding those who plotted against Caesar," Rabbi Babas remarked as he and the High Priest joined the conversation.

His eyes growing cold, Herod snarled, "My father was no traitor to the Empire."

Malchus took a bite out of the club sized leg of meat to avoid having to comment.

"I meant no disrespect, my lord," Babas said in a cold, condescending tone. "I merely intended to express my...regret that such rumors brought about his death. How did you manage to garner Rome's support under such awkward circumstances?"

"A persuasive tongue, no doubt," the High Priest remarked snidely, prompting the others to chuckle.

Unamused, Herod responded, "I assure you, my father was absolved of any wrong doing in their eyes. I saw to that, personally."

"Of course, he did," Hippicus said, deciding to lighten the mood. "Didn't you hear the king? He has his father's wit and his mother's charm. I've seen it, he can talk his way out of anything, this one." He glanced at Cypros across the room and remarked, "Too bad he didn't inherit her looks." They all chuckled.

****

Nahor, Babas' eldest son, glanced at Herod's sister, Salome. An eloquent beauty with raven black curls, sharp features and deep set eyes, she was dressed in an alluring long, black dress trimmed with gold and a teal veil. He remarked to his younger brother, Malachi, "Can you believe Herod's mother had the gall to name her daughter Salome after our queen."

"They're not even Jewish," Malachi murmured as he put his cup to his mouth."

"Shameful," their brother Dani murmured. "It's expected that King Hyrcanus would name his daughter Alexandra since his mother's name was Salome Alexandra, but many of the elders believe Cypros took the queens' first name for her daughter as..."

"A blatant attempt to make people think they are part of the royal bloodline, instead of glorified slaves," their brother Zachiah remarked as he joined them.

Nahor looked at him. "Is everything ready brother?"

Zachiah nodded. "Yes."

"Good. I shall inform father," Nahor replied. He glanced at Herod then said quietly to his brothers, "Dani, you wait by the window. I will signal you when things are quiet. Malachi, you and Zachiah go tell Simon to get ready, but stay out of sight." They nodded, and putting down their cups, headed outside.

****

"So, who is Emperor now?" King Malchus asked before tearing off another piece of meat with his teeth. "Some are saying Mark Antony, others say it is Octavian."

"Neither," Herod replied. "They and Marcus Lepidus have formed an alliance. Even now they are hunting for Caesar's assassins. After which, I am told, they plan to rule Rome together."

"Together!" King Malchus exclaimed as a few other guests joined them.

"Not exactly," Hippicus tried to explain as he attempted to steady the index finger he was waving before the Arabian king. He was so intoxicated he was swaying slightly and his speech was starting to slur. "In truth..." he said, putting his finger to his lips, as though he was spilling some big secret. "It's more like..." He looked at Herod.

Realizing his friend was too drunk to remember what he was talking about, Herod explained, "They plan to split the rule of the Empire."

"Yes, split it," Hippicus muttered, as he put the cup to his mouth. Herod took it away.

"You, my friend, have had enough for now." Turning his attention back to Malchus and the other guests, he continued. "They will divide it into three parts; each man will rule a region. From what I have been told, Mark Antony is expected to take Egypt and its surrounding areas."

"Does that mean he plans to rule over our lands?" the Arabian king murmured.

"We rule...gome roverns," Hippicus answered with a smirk. Everyone looked at him strangely. There was something wrong with his response, but he couldn't quite figure out what it was.

"What he means is, Rome governs," Herod corrected him.

"That's what I said." Hippicus muttered. Spotting a Persian dancer passing by, he announced, "If you will excuse me...I am in need of some...Persian...delicacies." Snickering, he sauntered off after the dancer, throwing his arm over her shoulder. "So...where are you from?" he asked, before sipping her cup of wine as they disappeared into the crowd.

"And what of Antigonus?" King Malchus asked, waving the half-eaten lamb leg around.

Spotting the princess mingling with the nobles across the room, Herod looked at the Arabian king and muttered, "Your highness, perhaps this is a conversation for another time." Before King Malchus could respond, Herod quickly dismissed himself and headed over to her.

"Princess...Miriam?" Herod said, walking up behind her. Upon turning around, he realized she was even more beautiful than he imagined.

"My lord, Herod. I did not get to thank you for rescuing us today."

"It was my pleasure." Holding one hand behind his back, he took her hand and kissed it. "I do not believe we have been formally introduced."

"Yet, I know you. I remember seeing you when I was a child."

"Then it is to my regret that I have been away from the capital so long, I did not recognize you. It seems in my absence, you have grown into a beautiful woman."

Miriam blushed.

****

Seth—whose name was actually Joseph, but to avoid confusion with his uncle Joseph, was aptly given the nickname Seth—had been working up the nerve to approach the princess. His arm bandaged up, he turned around only to discover that his brother, Herod, had beaten him to the chase. Frustrated, he stared at them and murmured. "Why does he always get all the beautiful women?"

"It's called charm," Joseph replied, placing his arm over the young man's shoulder. "And your brother has no shortage of it. Besides...you are not ready for a princess." Noticing a pretty dancer eyeing them as she passed, Joseph took Seth's wine and muttered, "You might try setting your sights a little lower, Nephew." He gulped down the cup of wine and handing it back to Seth, hurried off to catch up with the dancer. "And where are you from? You pretty little thing..."

Seth held up his cup as a servant refilled it, but before it touched his lips, his older sister Salome took it from him and put it to her lips. An eloquent beauty with raven black curls, sharp features and deep set eyes, she was dressed in an alluring long, black dress trimmed with gold and a teal veil. Observing Seth watching Herod and Princess Miriam, she jeered, "Too slow, little brother?"

"Better too slow than too old," Seth murmured, taking up another cup of wine from one of the servants.

"What are you talking about?"

Just then, the youngest of the four brothers, Pheroras, joined them. Looking at one another and smirking, Seth looked at his sister and replied, "I hear you are looking for another husband."

"Is that so?"

"Yes," Seth answered.

"It is true, you are planning to ask the king for his grandson's hand in marriage?" Pheroras asked.

Salome's lips curled into a cold smile. "Who told you that?"

"Does it matter?" Seth snickered,

"Tell me, Salome..." Pheroras asked, "Have you ever seen the king's grandson?"

"No, why?"

"You've been away from the capital too long." Seth turned around and gestured towards a triclinium behind them, where Princess Alexandra and the young prince were reclining.

Grinning from ear to ear, he leaned over and said quietly, "Salome, meet Prince Aristobolus III."

As Salome looked at the young prince, her smile faded. "He's a child!" She quickly turned around and murmured, "Curses!"

Pherorus looked at his brother and snidely remarked, "Do you think he likes older women?"

"Oh, shut up! I hate you both!" Salome hissed and walked off, while her brothers burst into laughter.

7

THE GAMES OF MEN

In a moment of quiet, Nahor signaled to his brother Dani with a nod. Dani then went out onto the terrace, and waiting until a pair of guards passed, took one of the torches posted on the wall, and waved it at his brothers who were watching from a dark alley facing the palace.

"That's the signal," Zachiah reported, "Go signal Simon." Malachi nodded and went to the street corner and made the sound of a dove with a particular song-pattern. The sound echoed through the streets being heard by Simon and a large crowd gathered in a square outside the palace gates.

Where a gentle flute playing in the background seemed to drown out the hum of all the chatter in the room, Herod and Miriam were chuckling like a pair of teenagers with their first crush on each other. Blushing, Herod started to remark, "I must admit...I..." The moment was spoiled by a sudden, loud and persistent chant, coming from outside.

"Down with the Half-Jews!!"

"And take your puppet with you!!"

"Down with the Half-Jews!!"

"And take your puppet with you!!"

Humiliated, Herod smiled and politely said, "Would you excuse me, Princess?" Promptly stepping aside, he met with Sohemus and quietly uttered, "Deal with it..."

"Gladly," Sohemus grunted. He had been itching to go shut them up.

Just as he moved off, Herod grabbed his arm and cautioned, "Discretely."

Sohemus nodded, and with a twisted grimace, signaled several of his men. They headed outside.

****

"This is our city!" Simon shouted from the top of a rock near the palace gates. "Yet those Half-Jews have the gall to sit in our Jewish palace celebrating their victory over us!!"

The crowd booed.

"They eat our food, drink our wine and rule our king! At least Antigonus had enough spine to stand up to them!!"

The crowd began to chant, *"Long live Antigonus!! Long live Antigonus!!"*

After quieting them down, he continued, "Herod and his brother are parasites!! And if we don't stop them, they will bleed us!!..." A large sword suddenly swung from behind and lopped off Simon's head mid-sentence. The crowd gasped and screamed as his body fell and his head rolled.

Sohemus then stood up on the rock, glaring at them. Horrified as they watched from the dark alley, Malachi drew a dagger and motioned forward, but his brother restrained him. "Now is not the time," he growled, pulling him back into the shadows.

Wiping the blood off his sword, he rested it against his shoulder and calmly asked, "Does anyone else have something to say?" The crowd stared in silence at him and his guards surrounding them. Sohemus lowered his sword and gruffly ordered, "Go home!! Or end up like him!" The crowd dispersed without hesitation, while Babas' sons took off. Sohemus looked at his men and pointing at the corpse, ordered, "Go dump that in the river." With a smirk, he headed back to the palace.

****

Herod promptly made his way back to the princess, being stopped along the way by the High Priest. "Lord Herod!"

"High Priest." He tried to glance over the High Priest's shoulder, noticing a few of the noble men circling the princess.

"I did not get a chance to congratulate you. It was quite the victory you led today. That arrogant prince has had the city in an uproar, cancelling some of our most important festivals...for months the temple has been short on wheat and grain...and..."

"You're point being?" Herod asked, growing anxiously annoyed.

"I was hoping we could discuss a measure of changes, starting with..."

"My lord...we are celebrating our king's victory over his enemy and the end of a 30-year war. I shall be happy to discuss whatever you wish...tomorrow." With that, he promptly stepped past the High Priest and made his way back towards the princess. Herod stepped into the midst of the group of men swooning around Princess Miriam and announced, "Your highness! Are you in need of rescue, yet again?"

Blushing, Miriam smiled and answered, "Yes, I believe I am."

"Then allow me." He took her by the hand and walked her out of the crowd of men. Knowing he was both a governor and general of the king's army, not a man dared challenge him. "Now...where were we?"

"I believe you were about to admit something?" Miriam replied with an alluring smile.

Herod chuckled and bashfully admitted, "I was going to say...I find myself smitten by your beauty." Seeing her blush, he took her hand and continued, "Might I..."

"Well...aren't you going to introduce me?" a voice rattled from behind him.

****

As Salome scoped the room for another potential prospect from a triclinium, one of the noble ladies named Aliyah joined her.

"Salome!"

Salome greeted her with an aloof smile. "Aliyah, how pleasant to see you cousin."

Aliyah smiled and hugged her before sitting down. "And you. I never thought this cursed war would end."

"I'm not sure it has. The people still refuse to accept my brothers as their governors."

"They're Jews! What do you expect?"

"Um. So, how are things in Galilee?"

Aliyah sipped her wine and with a heavy sigh remarked snidely, "Windy. The air smells like raw fish and salt."

"Sounds lovely." Salome continued scanning the room for a potential suitor.

"Are you as bored as I am?" Aliyah asked, glancing around the room.

Salome shrugged. "Not bored, simply exploring my prospects?"

"Ah yes, I forgot your first husband died. So tragic."

"Yes, it was."

"How did he die?"

Salome looked at Aliyah and replied coldly, "Poison."

Aliyah eyeballed her. "And now you look for another?"

"Yes."

"I wonder what he'll die of?" she muttered under her breath, reaching for a pastry shaped like a shell from a platter placed on the table by a servant girl.

"What was that?"

Aliyah stuffed the pastry into her mouth, and then looked at her cousin and shrugged, "Hum?" Rolling her eyes, Salome continued to scope the room. "Why are you looking for a husband?"

"Why not?"

"Because your brothers are governors. You are practically royalty. You are too valuable to choose your own husband. I am sure, one of your brothers plans to give you to some powerful ruler to secure an alliance. Do you not know powerful women are little more than pawns in the games of men?"

"You perhaps, but I shall make my own choice."

"Speaking of choice..." Aliyah spotted a ruggedly handsome Idumean commander—named Costobarus—looking their way. Cleaning off her mouth, she muttered, "I think I've made mine."

"Where?"

"There, by the window." As Costobarus looked away, Aliyah pointed in his direction and giggled. "Quite handsome, is he not?"

"Not bad, but he's a commander." Salome eyed him, making eye contact as he looked back in their direction.

Aliyah leaned in and chuckled excitedly. "Well, a commander is just what I need." She stood up and straightening her hair and clothing said, "Wish me good fortune."

Just as she started to move off, Salome sat up and grabbed her arm. "Wait! You cannot have him."

Aliyah looked back at her demanding, "Why not?"

Eyeing him seductively, Salome stood up and replied, "Because, he's mine."

"You just said you didn't want a commander."

"I've changed my mind."

"Well, too bad. I saw him first." Aliyah dragged her hand from her cousin and started to march towards him.

Slamming down her cup, Salome called after her in a venomous tone, "Do not think you exceed my brother's reach, cousin! I hear Herod is seeking an alliance with that overstuffed Arabian king, Malchus. He would never offer him his sister, but...his beautiful cousin to add to his royal harem...I am sure that would be enough to seal such an alliance. Don't you?"

Aliyah halted. She looked at the plump Arabian king, letting out a loud belch before continuing to sloppily stuff his face by the handfuls. After a moment of contemplating scratching out her cousin's eyes, she turned around with a pretentious smile and replied, "He's all yours, cousin."

"As long as he's not yours," Salome muttered, grinning smugly as Aliyah headed off in another direction.

****

Herod released Miriam's hand. Bearing an expression that was somewhere between a smile and a cringe, he turned around and looked down at the woman staring up at him. The woman—arrayed in a pale, yellow dress, trimmed with red and gold leaves and a purple vale—eyed Miriam coldly. Her demure appearance paled in comparison with the vivacious beauty of the princess.

"Princess Miriam, allow me to introduce...Doris." Doris gave him a cold smile, waiting for him to finish his sentence. "My..."

"There you are!" A commanding voice called from across the room. "I have been looking everywhere for you!" The crowd parted as Cypros marched towards them. Flaunting a beautiful violet dress with gold trim, and a violet silk vale beneath a crown of chestnut curls, Cypros stepped into their midst. Seeming to ignore everyone else, she peered down at Doris and said, "Your son has been crying for his mother for the last hour."

"The maids can attend to him," Doris replied, trying her best not to look intimidated.

"He does not want the maids. He wants his mother," Cypros insisted, glaring down at her with an iron stare.

Doris looked at Miriam and then at Herod for some support, but found none. "Don't you think I should...?"

"No. It has been a long day, and your son needs you. Perhaps you and he should retire for the night."

Lowering her eyes, Doris murmured as her expression hardened, "Fine." She looked at Miriam and sniped, "By the way...the man whose hand you were holding...he is my husband." Doris suddenly pulled Herod to her and kissed him passionately, then glared at Miriam before marching off, leaving them embarrassed.

Cypros watched her leave and grunted under her breath, "Not for long." She looked at Herod and muttered, "You know she only did that to embarrass you..."

Herod cleared his throat, trying to change the subject. Rubbing his brow and breathing out a stressful sigh, the governor explained, "Princess Miriam, this is my mother, Cypros."

"I know who you are," she said indifferently. "If you will excuse me." Her smile long faded, she put down her cup and walked away.

All Herod could do was watch her leave. He looked at his mother and murmured, "I suppose you are going to tell me I deserved that." He walked off, snatching a cup of wine from the tray of a passing servant.

"On the contrary..." his mother said, following him. "You deserve better."

"What?"

She also took a cup of wine and slipping her hand through his arm, walked with him. "Well look at you, Governor of Galilee and General of the king's army. Your father was famed for his wisdom and cunning on the battlefield, and you are twice the man he was. Not to mention tall and handsome, a fine catch for any women; yet you are married to some low-born, glorified..."

"Need I remind you, she is the mother of my child."

"She is an embarrassment," Cypros murmured, looking across at the High Priest and greeting him with a pretentious smile. "Why is it so hard for you to admit it?"

"Mother! Please!"

"How much land does her family own? Hum? A few vineyards in Galilee? Does her father wield any real power? No. She is a wasted opportunity, nothing more."

"She is my wife!" He escorted her to a vacant triclinium near the large marble pillar and sat down across from her.

"When these people look at you, Herod...what do you think they see?"

Herod shrugged. "A governor they hate?"

"Because you are an outsider trying to rule them. We will always be outsiders, but marriage to a Jewish princess..." She glanced at Miriam who was now trying to avoid eye contact with Herod.

"Marriage!"

"Please, spare me the look of shock, as if the thought had not entered your mind. I saw the way you looked at her." Cypros leaned her arm over the armrest adjacent to her son. "If you were to marry her, someday you could become king; your sons would be heirs to the throne, and you would bring the people to heel." She picked up a grape from the gold platter of fruit on the table before them.

Herod tossed back a mouthful of wine, savoring its bittersweet taste of fermented red grapes. Feeling it wash down his throat brought calmness to his mind. "You have everything so perfectly planned out, don't you? Except you are forgetting one thing..." He leaned forward and said, "I have a wife."

"Then why were you seducing the princess?"

Flustered, he fumbled for words. "I was just…"

"Divorce her," Cypros replied nonchalantly, as she tossed another grape into her mouth.

"What?"

"Divorce her," Cypros repeated, saying it slower with more emphasis.

"You want me to divorce my wife so I can marry another?"

"You're right…it would not look appropriate. You need to divorce and banish her."

Herod almost choked on his wine. "Banish!" He couldn't believe his ears. "And what of my son, Antipater? You expect me to banish him too?" Cypros just looked at him. "No! I will not abandon my son!"

"Have it your way…" she shrugged and looked up at King Hyrcanus. "How many times has the king lost his throne? A dozen. He never did have a stomach for war. That is why when reason failed, he gave his daughter to his brother's son, to bring about an alliance of peace. And now that he has his throne back, he wants nothing more…than peace. So, when Antigonus launches another attack—as he inevitably will—no doubt, the king will seek a peaceful resolution. What do you think that will be?"

Herod stared at her.

Cypros leaned forward and said sternly, "Then let me spell it out for you. To secure peace, the king will offer the usurper Princess Miriam's hand in marriage. And then you, my son, can settle for a life of mediocrity as the governor of some dusty town near the sea, where your name will be forgotten as you fade into nothingness, that's assuming your enemy does not have us all killed."

Herod glared at his mother, knowing exactly what she was doing. Annoyed, he banged his cup down on the table and getting up, growled, "I will not abandon my wife and son."

"Perhaps then, I shall discuss that matter with Phasael...or your brother Joseph. I am told, he has eyes for her." Herod halted for a moment, then walked off. Cypros popped another grape into her mouth and smiled to herself as she watched him.

****

At the crack of dawn, Pheroras started overseeing a large workforce tasked with the repairs of the gates and city wall while others continued to clear the streets of rubble and debris.

"I owe you. Judea owes you...a great debt," King Hyrcanus said, rubbing his hands over the smooth gold armrest. "You brought the Romans, you led the campaign...If not for you, our enemy would still be seated on this throne." He looked at Herod and asked, "How can I repay you?" Herod was standing by the window watching Princess Miriam and her maids make their way across the courtyard. As she disappeared inside the shadow of the bathhouse, he turned and looked at the king.

A few weeks later, Alexandra watched the High Priest tie a ribbon around Miriam and Herod's right hands, symbolically binding them together for their betrothal. Her mind trailed back to a conversation she had had with her father, when he summoned her to his chambers.

"No! Absolutely not!" Alexandra snapped, turning sharply to her father.

King Hyrcanus put down his cup and peered at her from across the table. "I was not asking your permission. He has made a request; I intend to honor it."

"But she is my daughter! Who she marries, should be my decision!"

"I am king! I will decide what is best for the kingdom."

"And you have decided that giving my daughter to this...Half-Jew is what's best for our kingdom?"

"Yes!"

"Have you forgotten, Father, they were our servants!"

"And now they are more powerful than us."

Alexandra got up, slamming her hands on the table. Startling the servants cleaning away bloodstains from the marble pillars and floors, and the stone walls leading out to the palace gardens. "That does not give Herod the right to demand my daughter's hand in marriage."

"Alexandra, be reasonable! Governor Herod is our strongest ally. If not for him, Antigonus would have killed you...and the boy, and then taken Miriam as his wife! Who better to marry her than Herod?"

"You know what he did to my husband and your brother!"

"Lies!" The king snarled, standing up. "Mere speculation by his enemies. Herod was nowhere *near that Roman camp when Alexander was executed!"*

"And what of your brother...he was poisoned!"

"And some say I am responsible! Do mere rumors make me guilty? Is that what you believe?"

Alexandra shook her head. "No, Father." She sighed heavily and calmly added, "But I do not trust Herod." She glared out at the gardens and scowled, "I do not trust him."

"Well, I do." The king gently squeezed her arms. "Joining our families is the best way to ensure our safety. If he wants Miriam, then he shall have her."

****

The gleeful grin on Cypros' face was enough to make Alexandra sick, almost as much as watching Herod kiss her daughter as the High Priest declared them betrothed. It seemed she wasn't the only one who disapproved of the union. Noticeably absent from the ceremony was Doris—standing in the shadows of an adjacent hallway, holding her son—she glared at Miriam with hateful eyes. Meanwhile, King Hyrcanus smiled politely and clapped, but his thoughts were elsewhere. Seeing Herod look over at Prince Aris, the king remembered how the conversation between he and Alexandra had ended.

"Tell me, Father...who is to be king after you? Herod or my son?"

Hyrcanus looked long and hard at Alexandra before replying, "Aris will be king after me."

8

PRINCE PACORUS

"So now that Half-Jew pig has stolen our beloved princess!" a Jewish leader named Judas shouted, as he stood over a group of Herod-haters gathered outside the palace gate. "What more is there left for him to take, but the throne? Will he now rule us as king?"

"NEVER!!!" the people roared in unison.

"Herod is a wolf in sheep's clothing! A glorified slave who knows nothing of love, only his own ambition! That Roman lover must not be allowed to marry our princess! Nor will he ever rule the Jewish people as king!!" The angry crowd vehemently agreed with him.

"I want that man arrested!" Herod scowled, staring down at them from the arched window of an upper hall.

"Now that you are betrothed to Princess Miriam, I thought they would surely embrace you," Cypros muttered, walking up behind him. "It seems I was mistaken."

"They love her, but hate me."

"They will come around." She rubbed his arm and reassuringly added, "When she gives you a son, you will be father to a Jewish prince, and then the people will endear you."

"I don't want their endearment," he grunted, moving from the window.

"Then what do you want?"

"Respect."

"And you shall have it," Cypros said, gently stroking his face. "They don't know you as I do, Herod. Give them time."

****

"It's time! For the real work to begin," Lucifer announced to his counsel, seated around a large luminous table made of black crystal. Turning his attention to an image of Herod and Miriam hovering above the center of the table, he explained, "Now that Herod holds power in one hand and love in the other...it's time to shift the balance; take his heart and carve it up piece by piece."

At the wave of his hand, *Destroyer* conjured up a map of the region surrounding Jerusalem. "And I know where to start," he said as the images, shifting like sand, shaped themselves into the royal palace of Parthia. "Antigonus is already seeking an alliance with the Parthians."

Lucifer smiled to himself. "What are you planning, you conniving prince?"

****

With the guards stationed by the ornate trellis windows, seated across from King Orodes, Antigonus picked up his cup. "So, we are agreed?"

The king who was dressed rather colorfully—baggy white cotton trousers; soft leather boots; a bright turquoise long-sleeved, three-quarter tunic with a gold belt wrapped around his extended belly—picked up his gold cup and smiled smugly, "Agreed. My son, Pacorus..." he gestured to his son, Prince Pacorus seated to his right, "...shall enter the city. He shall use his charm to convince Hyrcanus to join you at his camp, where he shall serve as mediator to negotiate a peaceful surrender."

"What if he fails to persuade them?" Antigonus asked. "What if he cannot enter the city?"

Prince Pacorus chuckled with a charismatic smile, "You leave that to me. Being altogether charming is what I do best. Besides, I am curious to see if the king's granddaughter is the rare beauty, men claim her to be."

The king put down his cup and leaning forward, asked, "Now...let us discuss, my price."

****

Miriam smiled gently as Herod whispered in her ear. He kissed her affectionately. "Be careful," she said softly, holding onto his hand as he moved off.

Herod kissed her hand and reassured her, "I will return soon." He moved on to Doris who had been holding his son and watching them jealously.

As Herod came and kissed his son, she asked, "Why must you go?"

"The men report that Antigonus has crossed our border with Parthian troops. I must march out against them before they reach the city."

Doris held onto his arm and quietly insisted, "Then send your brother, or one of the other commanders. It is the time of feasts. You know the people are threatening trouble."

"Phasael is not a man of war. His skills are better suited as governor. You will be safe, all of you. You have my word," he assured her, kissing her on her forehead. Though Doris had pursed her lips for a kiss, Herod moved off, stopping briefly to say goodbye to his mother. He bowed his head to King Hyrcanus and then headed for the doors, glancing at his brothers, Seth and Phasael. "Walk with me." They joined him as he walked down the long marble hall. "My men tell me they have seen an army of Parthians crossing our borders. It is no coincidence that they have chosen this time to invade. Rumor has it that Antigonus is with them."

"You believe he plans to use the feast as a means to enter the city?" Phasael asked.

"What better time..." Herod replied. "The gates will be open; thousands are expected to attend. If they disguise themselves and manage to hide among the visitors, the city will be overrun. Antigonus will take the throne from within our walls. We cannot allow that to happen."

"But how do you propose we stop him?" asked Seth.

As they reached the massive ornate doors at the entrance of the palace they stopped. "I will take a garrison of men with me and drive them back. Phasael, you stay; hold the city and guard the king."

"I will, Brother, but I should be going with you."

"No. The king will never hold the city without our strength."

Herod hugged his brother and ordered, "Triple the temple guards."

"Yes, Brother."

Herod then turned his attention to his younger brother. "Seth, I need you to take an envoy and head South."

"I am not going with you?"

"No. There is something I need you to do..."

Herod spoke quietly with his younger brother as Phasael headed back inside. Seth nodded and headed off while Herod climbed up onto his horse. He looked back and called, "Phasael! Keep the Parthians out of our city! At all costs! And whatever happens, do not trust them."

Herod's words rattled around in Phasael's head as he stood on the wall watching a sea of blue sashed Parthians riding towards the city after being rousted by Herod's troops. "Close the gates! CLOSE THE GATES!" he screamed. But by the time the guards managed to clear the travellers from the entrances, hundreds of vicious Parthian soldiers flooded into the city, riding through the crowded streets, slaughtering all in their path.

****

Some hours later, seated across a table, watching a servant girl top up Prince Pacorus' wine cup, Phasael pondered his brother's words, whilst gulping down his wine. He glanced across at King Hyrcanus. "So..." the king said, breaking the awkward silence. "You say you bring terms of peace?"

"Well, as you can see, I have already brought peace to your city," Prince Pacorus replied with a smug look.

"We had peace before your marauders raided our city and slaughtered our people on the holiest of our days!" Princess Alexandra lashed out, upon entering the throne room unannounced.

Slightly embarrassed, King Hyrcanus stood up and introduced them. "Prince Pacorus, may I present my daughter, the lovely Princess Alexandra."

Standing and nodding politely, Prince Pacorus responded, "It is a pleasure, Princess. And forgive me...my men were not acting under my orders, but simply retaliating to the attack governor Herod launched on them this morning."

Unimpressed, Alexandra eyed him distastefully and scowled, "Your men crossed our border allied with our enemy, what did you expect?"

Prince Pacorus eyed the guards around the room with their hands on their weapons, before replying smugly. "I did not come seeking war..."

"Then why have you sided with our enemy?" she demanded.

"Alexandra!" Hyrcanus growled, glaring at her.

"I merely stand here as a mediator," Prince Pacorus answered with a pretentious smile.

Humiliated by the princess, King Hyrcanus stepped before her and said sternly, "Prince Pacorus is our guest, and he has come with terms of peace. We will hear him out."

"As you wish, Father."

Guards opened the throne room door. Princess Miriam and Prince Aris walked in. Once the Parthian prince caught a glimpse of the beautiful princess, he could not take his eyes off her. "Allow me to present my grandchildren," King Hyrcanus said, gesturing to them, "Prince Aris III and Princess Miriam."

Barely acknowledging Aris, bright-eyed, Prince Pacorus took Miriam's hand. "Princess Miriam, I have heard of your beauty," he said, planting a kiss on her hand. Shifting his leering eye to her face, he remarked, "Yet, indeed the half was not told. You are truly..."

"Betrothed to Governor Herod," Phasael interjected.

Miriam smiled uncomfortably and withdrew her hand. It was evident he was entranced with her beauty. "The gods have smiled on you, great king."

The king held out his arms and extended them around Miriam and her brother. "The Almighty has indeed blessed me with riches beyond wealth."

"If you will excuse us Father, Governor..." And with a cold glance, Alexandra murmured, "Prince."

She looked at her children and gestured towards the door.

Pacorus watched them leave, and then with a sly smile, turned his attention back to the governor and the king. "Now...back to the matter at hand..."

****

"Who is he, Mother?" Miriam asked, as they stepped out into the hallway.

"Someone who cannot be trusted," Alexandra replied quietly. "Did you send for Ophellius?"

"I am here, my lady."

A tall, muscular, dark-skinned man dressed in light armor, and armed with a sword, greeted them at the entrance of the arched hallway. Head of the Royal Guards, and a trusted friend, Alexandra pulled him aside and said quietly, "I need you to leave immediately. Disguise yourself and find governor Herod, and give him this." She handed him a letter. "Warn him, that Prince Pacorus is here, and he is up to no good."

Ophellius took the letter. Disguised as a fruit merchant, he left the city, cutting the baskets loose the moment he passed the Parthian camp.

****

"So, the terms are simple..." Prince Pacorus continued as he carved off a chunk of seared lamb. "Prince Antigonus wishes to discuss terms of surrender. Now since I am sure...you, no more expect him to discuss these terms here, than he would expect you, at his camp. I suggest both parties meet at the camp of my commander—Barzapharnes. He has a small encampment on the Syrian border, less than 100 men. They are all loyal to me, not Antigonus. You want this war over? Accompany me back to his camp and hear the prince's terms. This war could be over by nightfall."

King Hyrcanus looked at Phasael. The trepidation was evident on their faces. "You want both the king and the governor to leave the safety of Jerusalem?" Hyrcanus asked.

Prince Pacorus put down his cup and leaned forward. "I want what you want—an end to the bloodshed. Look, bring as many soldiers as you like. You have my word: no harm will come to you or them. All I ask is that you hear him out."

****

"Fools!!" Herod snarled, slamming his cup down on the wooden table in his tent. "The Parthians have allied themselves with Antigonus, and my brother and the king welcome that scorpion—Pacorus, into the palace with open arms!"

"He did stop the Parthian attack on the city," Ophellius remarked, watching Herod.

"A ploy to gain my brother's trust! No doubt! While they spy out our weaknesses! How many Parthians entered the city?"

"100s, perhaps 1000s, but the prince ordered most to leave, save a few 100."

"You mean a few hundred spies! We are in the middle of a war, if I take my men from the battlefield now, the enemy will regroup and attack the city in full force. With troops, both within and outside our walls, we will be overrun. Our only hope is to keep them divided, drive the main army back across the border, then the rest will scatter."

"So, what are your orders, my lord?"

Herod sat down and quickly scratched out a letter. Sealing it with his insignia, he gave it to Ophellius with the stern warning, "Give this to Phasael and no-one else. Tell him, until I return to the city, do and say nothing beyond what I have instructed in this letter. Is that clear?"

"Yes, my lord."

"Good. Now go, quickly. I will bring reinforcement, as soon as I can." Ophellius nodded and headed for the entrance. Giving rise to a concern, Herod called after him, "Ophellius...post guards on my family. At the first sign of trouble, you get them to safety."

"I will, my lord." he nodded and headed out.

****

Upon arriving back at Jerusalem shortly after sunset, Ophellius found the palace surrounded by Parthian soldiers. He managed to slip past them, dressed as one of the servants. Once inside, the palace guards allowed him passage to the throne room where he barged inside with an urgent message for Governor Phasael. To his surprise, Alexandra was seated on the throne. She looked at him, despondent.

"My lady, why are there Parthian soldiers surrounding the palace?"

"Prince Pacorus left 200 men to guard against trouble. But clearly he means to make prisoners of us." Realizing Herod was absent, she asked, "Where is lord Herod?"

"He will be here with reinforcement..." Lowering his gaze, he added, "When the enemy is driven back."

Livid, Alexandra rose up and snapped, "When will that be? When our enemy has taken us prisoner! Or when my father is dead!"

"Where are the king and governor?"

She paced over to one of the windows and turned her gaze towards the northern hills. "He took them to Barzapharnes' camp, he said...to negotiate peace."

"But you do not believe his intensions are honorable?"

Alexandra looked at Ophellius and scowled wryly, "I believe that snake is leading them into a trap."

"I fear you may be right."

While Ophellius stumbled for words to comfort her, Alexandra looked at him and insisted, "Go after them, Ophellius."

"Governor Herod charged me with the safety of the royal house."

"Your first duty is to your king. My personal guard will watch over us, you take some men and you bring back the king."

Though reluctant to disobey Governor Herod, Princess Alexandra was right, as Head of the Royal Guard, his first duty was to the king. The commander nodded. He gathered a small squadron of guards, and under the cover of night, after slitting a few Parthian throats, they slipped out of the palace and left the city on horseback.

9

THE RICHEST MAN IN SYRIA

Ophellius and his men had spent the better part of the day tracking the Parthian party, stopping at every town, questioning every merchant and traveller they encountered to see which way they went. Their journey led them to a large town near the Syrian border where the servant of a man named Saramalla heard them asking about the Parthians. The servant led Ophellius and his men to the courtyard of an exquisite palace. While his men waited outside in the shade of palm trees, under the watchful eyes of armed guards, Ophellius and two of his commanders followed the servant inside. He led them down a wide white hallway of marble pillars and decorative arched windows, through a large reception hall, and out into a quiet courtyard, where Saramalla was having tea. The men waited by the entrance while the servant went over and whispered in his ear. Saramalla smiled and beckoned them to approach. "Welcome! Please, join me." Ophellius went over to the table, but his commanders remained at the entrance with their hands resting on the hilt of their swords, squaring off with the Syrian guards. "I am Saramalla, Governor of Syria."

"I know who you are, Governor," Ophellius replied with a marked look of urgency. "You don't walk into the palace of the richest man in Syria, and not know who he is."

"Indeed." Saramalla smiled bashfully. "May I offer you and your men some refreshments?" Before Ophellius could answer, Saramalla signaled his servants to come with refreshments.

"I thank you for your kindness, but we are here on a matter of urgency."

Saramalla's smile faded. "Yes, my servant tells me you are searching for the Parthian camp."

"The camp of Barzapharnes. You know where it is?"

"Nothing is traded here without my knowledge. I know where everything is. My merchants visit their camp every few days to sell them food and wares."

"Can they show us where it is?"

"Come with me." Saramalla led Ophellius and his commanders up to the roof of the palace. He pointed in the direction of a mountain range surrounding a valley that led to the ocean. "You see that winding valley leading down to the sea? Follow it, and you will find their camp down by the beach. But I must warn you, they have men hidden in the mountains."

"We were told there are only 100 men at the camp."

"A 100! Perhaps at the camp itself, but my men have reported seeing many more throughout the surrounding mountains."

"How many?"

Saramalla replied, "Perhaps 1,000. How many men do you have?"

"50."

"50!" Saramalla shook his head. "You and your men will never make it to the camp. They will pick you off like flies."

"We have to try."

"Why? What is so important in that camp that you and your men are willing to risk your lives for it?"

Ophellius eyed the old governor for a moment, and then answered, "Our king and governor."

"I see." Saramalla's servant helped him sit down. "Are they prisoners?"

Ophellius shrugged. "They could be."

"And you came with 50 men? And intend to go through those mountains?"

Ophellius glanced at his commanders; there was little, if any, optimism in their eyes. He looked at Saramalla and nodded. "Yes. Unless you have a better idea."

The Syrian governor looked up at him and smiled, "As a matter of fact...I do."

10

TERMS OF SURRENDER

The battle had been long and hard fought, but Herod and his army finally broke through the enemy line. They sent 10,000 of them fleeing across the border in a crushing defeat. The rest, both Parthian and enemy Jews, scattered to the hills and countryside. The incursion was over. Now, Herod set his sights on one thing...Jerusalem.

****

Ophellius glanced across at his commanders seated in one of the other boats. Saramalla had disguised all 50 of his men as merchants and sent them in small fishing boats, along with his tradesmen, to bring supplies to the Parthian camp. He had insisted it was the safest way to enter the camp without suspicion. Ophellius was not so sure.

As the men pulled their boats up onto the shore, Meshech—one of Saramalla's most trusted merchants—told Ophellius that one of his men reported seeing two men in royal apparel, being taken into one of the tents. "You see those two red tents?" he said, as they climbed out of the boats. "That's where he saw them." As the merchants picked up their baskets and headed off, Meshech and Ophellius started offloading their baskets filled with bread. He slipped him a dagger and warned, "If the soldiers catch you snooping around where you don't belong, they will kill you." He picked up another basket and as he put it down on the sand, gestured to a large tent close to the beach. "You see that tent over to the left, that's where they keep their weapons and armor. Disguise yourself as one of them, then you can move around the camp freely." He handed him a basket and moved aside the bread to show him a cloth in the bottom of the basket. Beneath it was a sack. "There are two changes of clothing inside. We will distract them. Get the king and governor changed and down to the shore. I'll have a boat waiting."

"Thank you, my friend." Ophellius nodded and headed off while the rest of his men spread out along the seashore with baskets and crates of food, clothing and wine. Each of them was concealing weapon under their cloaks. Upon Meshech's signal, a few of them started a rowdy argument that immediately drew the attention of the Parthians. The commotion allowed Ophellius to slip into the camp unnoticed. Moving cautiously among the tents, he headed straight for the armory, but upon spotting a pair of guards lingering near the entrance, he ducked behind a small tent. While he waited for the guards to move off, he heard snoring coming from inside. Peeping through a gap, he saw a soldier sleeping. He pulled out his dagger and slipped inside.

Ophellius crept up on the soldier, only to realize he was much bigger than expected. As he neared him, the soldier rolled over and stirring, opened his eyes. Startled, each stared at the other. The Parthian suddenly glanced at his sword and tried to grab it, while attempting to cry out, but Ophellius quickly cupped his hand over his mouth and stabbed him in the chest. The attack would have killed an ordinary man, but it seemed to have little affect on this brute. Ophellius pulled out the dagger and attempted to slash his throat, but the Parthian—unable to reach his weapon—grabbed his hand. He then clasped his beefy finger around Ophellius' throat and squeezed. The two struggled—Ophellius desperately trying to stab him in the neck while the Parthian squeezed his throat. They seemed to be at a stalemate. If not for wounding him in the chest, Ophellius would have stood no chance against the stocky enemy soldier, but as blood began to seep into his lungs, Ophellius could feel his grip weakening. Yet, it was not enough to free himself.

By this point, Ophellius was gasping for air. Realizing he was succumbing to his wound, the Parthian shifted his grip to Ophellius' jaw and began to twist his head to the right, in an attempt to snap his neck. Feeling his spine twisting, in desperation, the Jewish commander took his right hand from his enemy's mouth and used it to reinforce his grip on the blade. It was less than an inch from his neck.

Squealing from the pressure on his neck, with one final thrust, Ophellius kneed the Parthian in the groin. The moment he cringed, Ophellius threw his bodyweight onto his hands, plunging the dagger into the Parthian's neck. Blood began to gush out. The Parthian's grip remained firm for a moment, but choking on his own blood, his eyes rolled to the back of his head and his hands fell limply to the bed—much to Ophellius' relief. He leaned up, and catching his breath, retrieved his dagger. Blood poured out of the wound. Ophellius tried to roll the dead Parthian over to undress him, but he was too heavy and his garment was now soaked in blood. He started looking around. From what he could tell, there were a number of soldiers sharing the tent. Perhaps he could find another uniform among their belongings.

As he started to dig around, Ophellius heard voices outside. He hid behind the entrance. One of the men entered the tent. The moment he laid eyes on his dead comrade, he turned to alert the others. Instead, he ran into the Jewish stranger. Before he could cry out, Ophellius grabbed his head and twisted sharply, snapping his neck. A few minutes later he emerged dressed as a Parthian guard. Picking up the sack of garments, he headed over to the red tents.

****

Phasael, who had just sat down to eat, upon seeing a sword cut through the side of his tent and seeing someone slip inside, jumped up and called for his guards. Ophellius quickly tried to calm him. "Governor, it's me, Ophellius." He took off his helmet.

"Ophellius?" Phasael stared at him bewildered. One of his personal guards entered. "It's alright," Phasael reassured him. "Wait outside, and inform me before anyone comes." The guard nodded and exited, leaving the two men alone. Turning his attention back to Ophellius, Phasael asked, "What are you doing here?"

"My lord, you and the king are in grave danger."

"What do you mean, in danger?"

Ophellius handed Phasael the letter his brother had sent for him. "Lord Herod ordered me to give you this."

Seeing his brother's seal unbroken, Phasael opened the letter and read it. "He says I should imprison Pacorus and drive out the Parthians." He looked at Ophellius and murmured, "It's a little late for that, don't you think?"

"By the time I returned to the palace, you had already left."

"You went to see Herod?"

"Princess Alexandra suspected the prince of treachery. She sent me to lord Herod to seek his advice."

"Alexandra?"

"Yes, my lord. She feared for you and her father, and sent me here with 50 men to safeguard you back to Jerusalem."

"We came with an escort of 200 men, and there are less than 100 Parthian soldiers at this camp."

"There are more than 1,000 hiding in the mountains surrounding here. The Syrian governor, Saramalla showed me."

"He showed you this?"

"Yes, and one of his men overheard the guards boasting. They said that Antigonus has offered the Parthian Prince and his father 1,000 talents of gold and 500 of our noble women in payment for the capture of you, your brother and the king."

"No. That cannot be true!"

"It is, my lord. Prince Pacorus has led you both into a trap. He and Barzapharnes intend to kill you and Governor Herod."

Phasael looked at him puzzled, "What you are saying makes no sense! They have welcomed us as honored guests, not captives. No honorable man would murder his guests!"

"These men have no honor, my lord. You and the king are both in grave danger. But I have a plan of escape. We have boats on the shore, and Governor Saramalla has a merchant ship waiting to take us to safety." He took out the bundle of clothes. "I have brought you merchant garments. My men are among Saramalla's merchants, down on the beach. Change, and I will escort you both back to the shore. Where is King Hyrcanus?"

"He is in Barzapharnes' tent."

"Can you get him out without arousing suspicion?"

"No. Besides, if what you say is true, then our escape may lead to Herod's capture. I have a better idea. Wait here until I return."

Before Ophellius could protest, Phasael left the tent. Followed by two of his bodyguards, he marched over to Barzapharnes tent. Ordering his men to wait outside, he barged in.

"Governor?"

"Whose idea was it?" he demanded, interrupting their meal.

Barzapharnes looked at Phasael puzzled and asked, "What idea?"

"Dragging us out here, in the middle of the desert? Using us as bait? When exactly did you plan to kill us?"

"What!!" King Hyrcanus stood up, startled. His bodyguards drew their swords and immediately stood before him. Barzapharnes' guards also drew theirs.

"What are you talking about?" Barzapharnes asked, looking both startled and offended.

Phasael looked at Hyrcanus and remarked, "Did you know your nephew offered Prince Pacorus 1,000 talents of gold and 500 of our noble women to lure us out here, away from the safety of the palace, so he can depose of you and me, and then kill Herod!"

"What!!" almost stumbling over his chair, King Hyrcanus glared wide-eyed at Barzapharnes.

Standing up, straightening his breastplate, he stuttered, "Who...who has been filling your head with these lies?"

"Do not deny it!" Phasael growled angrily, watching Barzapharnes fumbling as he poured himself another cup of wine. "We came here in good faith, seeking peace! And you would repay our good will with treachery? That is the action of cowards!"

"We have welcomed you and your men and..."

"Commander, I have neither the time nor patience for any more lies!" Phasael snapped. "You go and tell Prince Pacorus, whatever Antigonus has offered him, if he grants us safe passage back to Jerusalem, I will double it."

His offer was met with cold silence. Barzapharnes swallowed hard, then put down his cup and said, "Wait here." Without even a glance in their direction, and his guards following, the commander stepped outside and looked across at the Parthian soldiers stationed near the Judean guards. He brought his hand up into the air, balled it into a fist and aggressively brought it down. That was the signal. A horn was sounded. The Parthians immediately drew their weapons and started slaying the Judeans, while more began to emerge from the surrounding hills and mountains and joined the attack.

Barzapharnes' guards slew the king and governor's guards stationed outside his tent. Hearing the ruckus, the king's bodyguards tried to lead them out of the tent, but the moment they reached the threshold, they were picked off by archers. Several Parthian soldiers with drawn swords then forced them back inside. "What is the meaning of this?" the king demanded. One of the guards stepped aside, showing them their slain Judean guards, lying in the dirt.

Standing guard at the governor's tent, when the attack started and more Parthian soldiers stormed the camp, realizing there was nothing he could do to help the Judean guards, Ophellius opted to save the king and the governor. Ignoring the cries of his comrades, he drew his sword and marched towards the commander's tent.

As he neared the entrance, Ophellius heard King Hyrcanus shriek from inside, "Unhand me!!"

The Jewish commander stepped over the bodies by the entrance and marched in. Since he was dressed as a Parthian, the six soldiers holding the king and governor prisoners, paid him little attention until Ophellius thrust his sword through the back of one, then quickly spun around and slashed the throat of another. Startled, the others—realizing what was happening—released the prisoners and attacked him. One swung at his head. Ophellius ducked and sliced open his gut. With marked skill, he cut off the arm of the fourth before thrusting his sword through his chest, then spun and cut the hamstring of the fifth, and with amazing speed, decapitated both him and the sixth guard with two quick swipes. He did it all within less than a minute. "Come with me. They are killing everyone. Your only hope is to get to the shore." He picked up a couple of blankets from the commander's bed, and tossed them to the king and the governor. "Cover yourselves and follow me! We can escape with the merchants."

Without protest, both men threw the blankets over their shoulders like shawls to conceal their royal apparel while Ophellius cut open a hole in the back of the tent. They all slipped out, relatively unnoticed and headed for the beach.

Mere steps away from freedom, Ophellius suddenly stopped cold. Trails of food, garments and overturned baskets were strewn across the soft white sand, amidst puddles of blood. Merchants lay dead, and those trying to flee to their boats were being slain by arrows and spears. Most of his men were either dead or engaged in battle with the Parthians, but vastly outnumbered, they stood little chance. His heart sunk. Ophellius had hoped that the fighting had not reached the beach. Whether the Parthians had discovered the Judeans among the merchants or simply just decided it was too risky to let anyone escape, they were slaughtering everyone. Ophellius saw Meshech running for his boat. He directed Phasael and Hyrcanus to follow, but when a spear struck Meshech in the back, the men halted. "There's no escaping that way," Ophellius called.

Phasael spotted some horses. "There! We can escape by horse."

Just as they turned to run towards the horses, they found themselves facing a group of Parthians running towards them. With the enemy in front and behind, their escape route was cut off. Ophellius took a stance, ready to defend them until the end, but in an unexpected move, Phasael whispered, "No, you can't help us if you are dead." He knocked Ophellius down and threw off the blanket revealing his royal garments. "Go, warn Herod," he said before throwing up his hands in surrender. Seeing that there was no way for them to escape, Hyrcanus did the same. He looked at Ophellius and discretely nodded.

Assuming he was one of them, the Parthians closed in around the prisoners, ignoring Ophellius. Weighing his chances of mounting a successful rescue—as zero to one—Ophellius watched the Parthians escort the king and the governor back to Barzapharnes and Prince Pacorus. With his men all lying dead on the beach, there was nothing he could do to save them, except get help.

Reluctantly, he headed for the horses. Seeing the guards bringing them to their knees, Ophellius rode out of the camp just as Prince Antigonus emerged from one of the tents. A smug grin on his weasel face, he strutted towards the king and said smugly, "Greetings Uncle. My apologies. It seems Prince Pacorus neglected to tell you that we are not here to discuss terms of my surrender, but yours."

11

THE TRAP

Upon arrival at the palace, to his dismay, Herod discovered that his brother and the king—against their better judgment—had left Jerusalem and accompanied the Parthian Prince to his camp. Shortly before dusk, he received a message that Prince Pacorus had arrived, and was seeking an audience with him. With his troops waiting outside, the prince—escorted by an armed envoy—entered the throne room with open arms and a pretentiously broad smile. "Lord Herod!"

Seated on the throne with Sohemus and Hippicus on either side, Herod glared at the prince. He greeted him with an icy smile. "Prince Pacorus. It is a surprise to see you. What brings you here, at this hour?"

"I wanted to congratulate you on your victory. I hear you drove my army back across the border." Despite his smile and coy tone, his eyes were sinister and cold.

"Pity you were not there to witness it," Herod said, in an equally loathsome tone. "Might I offer you some wine?"

Several servants rushed in with wine and refreshments for the governor and his uninvited Parthian guests. Convinced it might be poisoned, Prince Pacorus glanced at the wine then looked at Herod and replied, "No. But feel free to indulge."

"Well, surely you did not travel all this way just to congratulate me on your defeat, so why don't we get down to why you are really here? You would not dare step foot in our city if you did not have my brother and our king as hostages!"

"Hostages!" Looking smugly offended, Prince Pacorus shook his head and nonchalantly replied, "You mean guests." He strolled around the throne room, admiring its many ornate gold furnishings.

"Guests? Last I heard…they were prisoners."

Pacorus eyed him, and tapping his index fingers together, replied innocently, "Prisoners! Where did you hear such a preposterous rumor? King Hyrcanus and your brother were invited to participate in negotiations, to bring about a peaceful resolution to this war, which I and my people have been dragged into."

"Dragged into?" Herod chuckled to himself as he stepped down from his throne. Resting his hand on his weapon, he made his way down the steps. "So, tell me, what kind of negotiations did you lure them into?"

Cupping his hands behind his back, the prince smugly answered, "Terms of surrender."

"Yours or ours?"

Prince Pacorus looked at him and chuckled. "Perhaps your king should have asked that question before accepting our invitation."

Nearing the prince, Herod's smile suddenly faded into a fierce scowl; he drew his sword and shoved the blade against Prince Pacorus' throat. The prince's guards immediately drew their weapons, as did Sohemus and Hippicus. The prince ordered, "Stay your weapons!" His men halted.

"Give me one good reason why I shouldn't just slaughter you where you stand!"

"I'll give you two," Pacorus replied fearlessly. "Kill me and you sign their death warrants.

Antigonus will send pieces of them to every tribe in Israel."

Herod narrowed his eyes. "So now you threaten their lives?"

"No Herod..." Pacorus snarled, "you do. They are guests, free to leave whenever they choose...Providing I return...unharmed."

The two glared at one another until Herod lowered his sword and stepped back. "Forgive me. I was sure they were your prisoners."

"Well..." Prince Pacorus replied, feeling his throat. "If you doubt my words, perhaps you should come and see for yourself."

Herod nodded, "Perhaps I will...tomorrow."

Prince Pacorus responded wryly, "Then I will leave a small escort to guide you to their location."

"You are most...gracious," Herod said, forcing an icy smile.

"Well, tomorrow, then," the prince said, with a nod of his head.

His eyes like daggers, Herod nodded as the prince and his party headed for the door. "Tell my brother, I will see him soon," he called.

"I will be sure to." The prince looked back and with a nod, headed out.

Once the door closed, Herod ordered his guards to leave. Ophellius stepped out from the shadows. "He's lying, my lord, I saw him capture them with my own eyes."

"Why did you let him go?" Sohemus growled, gripping the hilt of his sword.

"If Pacorus does not return, they may not kill the king—not yet, but they will kill my brother. I am sure of it." Herod strolled over to the window overlooking the palace gate.

"And now he seeks to capture you as well," Hippicus cautioned.

Herod watched Pacorus and his men leave.

As soon as they stepped through the gates, the arrogant prince uttered to his commander, "The moment Herod leaves the city, kill him. Bring me his head and his women. Tomorrow, we attack the city and declare Antigonus king."

Herod stepped away from the window and remarked, "Alexandra says her spies saw his troops hiding in the hills."

"They intend to ambush you tomorrow," Ophellius warned. "You will never reach their camp alive."

Herod breathed a heavy sigh and murmured, "Of that I have no doubt."

"If you stay, they will attack the city..." Sohemus grumbled. "If we resist..."

"They will kill my brother. And if we surrender?" Herod pondered aloud.

"They will kill you both; throw your sons and brothers from the walls, and take your wives and daughters as slaves," Sohemus answered in a somber tone as he glared out across the landscape."

"What are you both talking about?" Hippicus exclaimed, frustrated. "We have Jerusalem! He has a few thousand troops; we have an army of tens of thousands! Ophellius knows where their camp is; I say he and I leave tonight and lead a rescue party—wipe out those Parthians dogs! Bring back your brother, the king and that bastard's head! While you and the rest of our army defends the city!"

"I agree!" said Sohemus, geared up for war.

"Well I do not!" Cypros remarked, entering the throne room. An advisor named Althazar followed her in. "That plan would be all well and good...if the people were on your side!"

"Mother..." Herod said, meeting her halfway, "It is inappropriate for you to..."

"To what? Advise my son..." she sniped, stepping past him, "Who is about to take the advice of two half-wit commanders..." She glanced at Sohemus as she strutted towards Hippicus. "One a mindless brute, and the other a whoremonger who spends his time indulging in whores, wine and...God knows what else." Staring Hippicus down until he lowered his head, she shifted her gaze to Herod, and then continued, "And they think that qualifies them to give advice to a governor on matters of which they know nothing."

"I know of war," grunted Sohemus.

"Perhaps, but you know nothing of politics. I was married to the king's Chief Advisor—a general whose strategic skills were renowned across the Roman Empire! I was discussing war and politics when you were still an itch in your father's...."

"Mother!" Herod snapped, interrupting her. "Why are you here?"

Turning her attention back to her son, Cypros gestured to the advisor. "Tell him what you know, Althazar."

The timid advisor stepped forward and explained, "It seems rumors have circulated throughout the city that the king has been taken captive by his nephew Antigonus. No doubt these rumors were started by the Parthians to bring about panic and discourse among the people."

"Your point being?" Herod asked.

Glancing at Cypros for reassurance, Althazar said hesitantly, "The people...are..."

"The people blame you for the king's capture," Cypros snapped, impatiently.

"What! But I had nothing to do with it!"

"Perhaps so my lord, but that is not what the people are saying," Althazar insisted. "They say it is because you took our troops and left the city undefended that the Parthians were able to capture the king."

Enraged, Herod surged forward, barking, "That's NOT TRUE! I left to defend our city!" Althazar retreated behind Cypros as Herod growled, "There were more than enough troops to stop the incursion! I warned Phasael not to trust them!!..."

"Calm down," Cypros insisted, pressing her hand against his chest. "It's too late now for blame."

"But the people blame me!"

"And that is why we cannot stay here," Cypros said calmly.

"What?" Herod looked at his mother bewildered.

She glanced at Althazar, who continued from a safe distance. "It does not matter who is to blame, my lord, if the king is not here for the people to rally around, they will look to the next best thing. The fact remains...Prince Antigonus is a Jew of the royal bloodline, and you...are not."

"So?"

Lowering his head, Althazar remarked, "In the event of a war, without King Hyrcanus at your side, the people are more likely to hand you over to the Jewish prince than fight against him with...a Half-Jew."

"WHAT!!" His hand on his sword, Herod lunged at the advisor, but his mother held him back.

"Those are not his words!" she said forcefully. "He simply echoes the words of the people."

"What about Prince Aris? Or Princess Alexandra?" Hippicus suggested.

"The boy is too young to lead us into war, and they will not follow a princess without a husband to lead the charge," Althazar replied.

Looking up at her son—seething, as he stared out at the city lights flickering in the evening sky—Cypros gently ran her hand from the worried lines on his brow to his cheeks, and softly called, "Herod! We cannot stay here: it's not safe. They will not harm Alexandra or her children, but they will turn us over to Antigonus. We must flee Jerusalem."

Her words sinking in, Herod turned his gaze to his mother and insisted, "I'm not leaving Miriam. And Prince Aris is the heir to the throne; if he stays, Antigonus will kill him—and if he must—he'll marry Alexandra to secure his rule. The boy and his mother cannot stay either. If anything happens to King Hyrcanus, Prince Aris is our only hope of reclaiming the throne."

"Then it is settled, we all leave the palace." She gave him a reassuring smile and ordered,

"Now, I will gather all those in the royal household; you get those two half-wits to rally yours troops, and Althazar will gather the noble houses loyal to you, then let us leave the city under the cover of night."

Just as she started to walk off, Herod caught her by the arm and asked, "Mother...do you blame me for the capture of Phasael and the king?"

Fighting back her tears, Cypros gently stroked his cheek and said, "Of course, I don't."

"I warned him," Herod murmured, pining. "Phasael should have known better than to trust that...scorpion!"

"Your brother is weak; far too trusting. I have always said that. I told your father, he does not have your strength or your wisdom. He never should have made him governor of Jerusalem; that should have been you." She wiped away a tear rolling down his cheek. "You cannot blame yourself for your brother's mistakes, or your father's failure. But now, Herod, you must be strong...for all of us." Herod nodded. Wiping away her own tears, Cypros smiled and said, "Go get ready to lead us out." She headed for the door and called over her shoulder so the others could hear,

"And leave the advice to the wise and experienced!"

12

SAND

Beneath a blanket of turbulent clouds, gargoyles circled the grey skies like vultures over a fresh carcass. It was the red mist washing over the vast landscape that drew them. The blood of the slaughtered was saturating the earth while the cries of their souls, being dragged down to hell, carried on the wind like a howling symphony of moans—music to the Devil's ears. He stood atop a high peak, surveying his kingdom—man's kingdom.

Hearing a heavy thud on the crags behind him, Lucifer remarked, "I trust you bring me good news?"

Destroyer approached, folding in his black wings. "The Parthian Prince has troops scattered throughout the hills. He has cut off every route and placed guards at every gate of Jerusalem. He plans to kill Herod."

Lucifer looked over at *Destroyer* and murmured, "He is of no use to me dead."

"What would you have me do?"

"You...will do nothing. This calls for something more...creative." With a parting look, Lucifer fell backwards off the ledge. Falling in a rapid descent, he opened his arms and with a sudden fiery flash of light, disappeared.

****

Herod's commanders and Advisor had managed to rally around 9,000 people of whose loyalty to him was unquestioned, including: soldiers, guards and their families; mercenaries; members of several noble houses and many others who supported him. As he, his commanders and advisors stood around a table looking at a map of the city, deep in thought, Herod moved off and peered out the window. Most of the others were too deep in discussion to notice, but Hippicus and his uncle watched him with concern. Although he had only a fraction of the Judean army, Herod still desperately deliberated mounting a rescue attempt of his brother and the king.

"You still want to get them out, don't you?" Joseph asked quietly as he approached him.

Herod breathed a heavy sigh. "It's too risky. We don't have enough men, nor do we know how many reinforcements may have joined the Parthian camp."

"But what if we could save them?" Hippicus insisted quietly, joining them. "We drove most of the Parthians back across the border, the rest are scattered throughout the hillsides. Even if Antigonus has a few thousand men, so what? We've faced greater odds and won."

"Marching into battle with the royal family is not an option," Herod objected.

Joseph agreed with him, adding, "And dividing our ranks would only increase our chance of being captured."

"Besides...there is no guarantee we can save the king or Phasael..." Herod remarked with a heavy sigh. "We don't even know if they are still alive."

"But Herod..."

"No!" Herod snapped sharply. "I will not risk the lives of my family on a futile mission!" The room grew silent. He looked around at the others and said, "Neither man would want that." He glanced at his mother, who nodded as he stated, "We have no other choice...we save ourselves and the royal family. Now...let's devise a plan of escape." He headed back to the table and looked at the map. "How many Parthians are surrounding the city?"

"Hundreds, perhaps thousands, and more in the hills," Sohemus reported. "They have men stationed at every gate around the city; they are heaviest around the palace and the temple walls."

"Because that is where he believes we will try to mount our escape," Cypros observed.

"How many people did you say we have?" Herod asked.

"Over 9,000, my lord," Althazar replied.

Looking around at everyone, Herod asked, "So, the obvious question is...how do we get 9,000 people out of the city unnoticed?"

****

In a flash of searing red light, Lucifer landed on the top of a hill overlooking Jerusalem. Dusk was descending. The indigo sky was awash with a deep burst of red and amber splashed across the horizon. In the distance, mountains were becoming silhouettes against the vibrant backdrop, while Jerusalem gleamed like a gem, amidst the tattered Parthian tents and campfires scattered across the plains.

Surveying the landscape, Lucifer saw Parthians hiding among the hills for miles around. He stooped down and picked up a handful of sand. Looking up into the cloudless sky, he inhaled a deep breath and pursing his lips, blew the sand right across the landscape. He watched it dance on the wind before slowly dispersing east; then he waited.

A moment later, a sudden strong wind began to howl. It grew stronger and louder until it became a deafening roar, drawing hundreds of Parthian soldiers out of their tents. Though none could see the dark shadowy figure standing on the hill in the dim light, they saw a thick cloud rising over the horizon. Like the swell of a giant wave riding the ocean, a violent sandstorm rolled over the hills, sending the soldiers into a panic. They barely had time to run, before the blistering storm enveloped the camp, blinding them in a cloud of sand and debris. With the course sand grating their skin, making it impossible to see and difficult to breathe, most ran for shelter within their tents, while a few covered their faces and attempted to save their animals.

****

Upon hearing a distant roar, Salome looked outside, "A sandstorm!"

Herod and his mother were standing at the window, looking out at the sky. The sandstorm had rolled in just as they were preparing to depart. The worst of it seemed to be concentrated on the hills and the plains around the north and eastern side of city where it had completely engulfed the enemy camp.

"We're in luck," Cypros remarked. "The timing could not have been better."

"How so?" asked Herod.

"The sandstorm has blinded our enemy," she replied, heading back to the table.

"It has also blinded us," Herod remarked.

"But we know the land; they do not."

"It makes no difference, we could ride right past the enemy or we could end up in their camp," Joseph commented. "No-one can travel through a sandstorm, all you can do is wait it out."

"We cannot wait!" Herod said, his mind churning wildly, seeking a solution. "My mother is right. We needed a way to get our people out...this is it. The question now is...how?" He looked at

Althazar. "Well, Advisor...advise me. How do we make our escape?"

After studying the direction of the winds and returning to the map, Althazar pointed to one of the gates. "Our best escape may be through..."

At that moment, Pheroras burst into the room. "Brother! Come with me!" He pulled a cloth over his face and pushed open the shutters of the terrace door. The wind began to blow a light sputter of sand inside, but he looked back and said, "You'll never believe this!" As Herod and the others joined him out on the terrace, Pheroras pointed south. "The storm surrounds the city, but the way south...look at it, it's clear enough to see the mountains."

Holding a cloth over his face, Herod patted him on the back and rejoiced, "It seems God made a way!"

"Here! My lord..." Althazar called, leading them back to the map. He pointed to a southern gate. "We know at least half their forces have been blinded by the storm. At best, the rest will be scattered. They cannot send for reinforcements. So, as I was going to suggest...we take the Essene gate. We can dispense of any enemy troops we encounter. Once we are clear of the wall, we make our way down to the Hinnom valley.

"And pray the wind doesn't change direction," Sohemus remarked snidely.

Nodding, Althazar continued, "We will be leaving under the cover of night, as well as the sandstorm. The hills will shield us from the storm, the valley will steer our direction, and should the storm break, the shadows will conceal us from our enemy."

Herod nodded. "Agreed." He looked up at the others and ordered, "We travel throughout the night, get as far away from here as we can, and then we head south. Tell the men to move out. And kill any Parthians they see."

****

Althazar was right, it didn't take much for Herod's troops to overpower the Parthian guards at the southern walls and gates. They were so busy trying to shield themselves from the sand and wind, Herod and his troops caught them by surprise. The few who did manage to escape, rode into the storm, and never re-emerged. Herod and his family, along with the royal family and all those loyal to him, managed to escape the city unscathed.

While many, like Cypros, believed the sandstorm and the clearing to be a stroke of good luck, they might have thought differently had they seen or known the plans of the tall shadowy figure hiding in the storm watching them as they passed by.

13

THE COWARD'S WAY

By morning, the storm had long subsided, and though buried beneath sand, the Parthians had managed to dig themselves out.

With first light came the arrival of Prince Antigonus and his Parthian army. Joined by Prince Pacorus, he led a charge against the city only to find the gates opened and the palace deserted. Everyone loyal to Herod from soldiers and mercenaries to servants and nobles had left with him, during the night. All except, that was, Itiel who had been stranded in the temple by the sandstorm, and returned to find everyone gone.

****

Herod looked back at Miriam and Doris and smiled. Doris paid him little attention, but despite forcing a smile, the sadness was evident in Miriam's eyes. He looked past them to the long line of people, horses, and carts, following him. He, Sohemus, Hippicus and his uncle Joseph were leading the convoy through the twisting valleys heading south with an armed escort of soldiers, guards and mercenaries guarding them every step of the way. "All 9,000 made it out of the city?" Herod asked.

"At last count, yes," Sohemus replied, steering his horse slightly to the left to avoid a small rock in their path.

"And I think a few hundred more have joined us along the way," Joseph remarked.

"I didn't think so many people liked you," Hippicus joked.

Herod smiled. "Neither did I."

"How do you expect to feed them?" Sohemus asked. "With this many mouths, we'll be out of food in a matter of days."

"I wont turn them away," Herod insisted. "Better they fight with me, than against me. To send them back, is to send them into the arms of my enemy."

"Sohemus, you are only thinking of your belly," Joseph joked.

"Does he think of anything else?" Hippicus jeered. They all laughed.

"You jest? You see this?" Sohemus showed them his beefy muscles. "I'll be picking my teeth with your bones, long before I starve."

"Don't worry, they'll be plenty of food, where we're going."

"And where is that?" asked Joseph.

"Idumea."

****

After being welcomed back into the city by his loyalist, Antigonus headed down the stone steps leading to the treasury located in the palace. Finding it unguarded and unlocked, he barged inside.

The massive room with its vaulted ceilings, normally filled with treasure, was all but empty. "No, No!" Antigonus murmured as he staggered around the room searching the few empty chests they'd left behind. Finding only a few trinkets and 300 shekels of gold, he sunk to his knees and shrieked, "NOOO!!!" His cry resounded throughout the palace, drawing several guards. Prince Pacorus—followed by Barzapharnes, pushed past them, finding the new king on his knees.

Antigonus looked up at him and moaned, "It's gone!"

"What's gone?"

"The treasure, the gold! Herod's taken it all!!"

Prince Pacorus grabbed the king and dragged him to his feet; both their guards drew weapons against one another. "I promised you the throne in exchange for gold, noble women and a princess! I see no women, no princess and now you tell me, there's no gold!"

"He took everything! All I have are 300 shekels of gold."

Enraged, Pacorus slapped the coins from his hand and shoved him away. "I delivered you the city! Now I want my gold, and my women!! And you are going to give it to me or my men will ransack every town and city in Judea until I have what I was promised!!" In a rage, he stormed off towards the door and ordered, "Take everything!" then he barked at Barzapharnes, "Send out troops! Scour every hill! Search every town! I WANT HEROD FOUND!!"

"Wait!!" King Antigonus clambered to his feet. "You want the princess and the gold! I want Herod's head! I know how to we can get them both!" Shifting a glance at the palace guards, he ordered, "Bring me the prisoners!"

****

"So, where is the gold?" Joseph asked, throwing a glance in Herod's direction. "I know you didn't just leave it for that swine of a prince."

Before saying a word, the smug look on Herod face told him everything he needed to know. "I sent it to Idumea."

"Before the Parthians even invaded?" Hippicus smirked. "You, sly fox."

"I know my brother," Herod replied. "I couldn't trust him or the king with it, not with the Parthians at our borders. I thought they might use it to pay them off, so I sent it away with Seth, the morning I left for battle." His smile slowly faded into a heavy sigh. "All things considered...perhaps, I should have left it."

"You think Prince Pacorus would have taken your money and left?" Sohemus asked sarcastically. "The man has no honor!"

"Sohemus is right," Joseph stated, taking a swig of wine from his wineskin before handing it to Herod. "If you had left the gold, right now, the Parthians would have it and your brother."

"And the king," Hippicus added. "You made the right decision. Isn't that right, Advisor?" he called to Althazar. He and Pheroras were riding behind them alongside the wagon with Herod's mother and sister.

"Indeed," Althazar answered.

Hippicus smirked and took the wineskin as Herod handed it to him, then tossed it over to Sohemus.

"My lord, might I ask where we are going?" Costobarus asked. He was riding on the other side of the wagon, amusing himself with Salome's attempts to ignore him.

"Idumea," Herod replied. "We'll be safe there."

"My home," Costobarus remarked, glancing at Salome and smiling.

"What do you find so amusing?" she asked.

"You, pretending you don't see me looking at you," he answered.

"Of course, I see you. I just choose to ignore you," she replied with a snobby look.

"And why is that?"

Salome shrugged. "Why not. It's not like you're a prince or a king. You're not even a nobleman, just a runt in my brother's army, and I don't talk to such rabble."

"Rabble? Is that what I am?" he said with a sarcastic smile. "That's funny, I could have sworn my father was a priest of the Idumean Temple, and my mother of noble blood, and yet, they somehow managed to give birth to rabble. Hum?" Before Salome could respond, Costobarus rode off with a smug grin, to check on his men further back, leaving her wide-eyed and open-mouthed.

Pheroras rode up alongside her and jeered, "First you pick one that's too young, and then you insult a high-born...at this rate, Sister, you'll be an old woman before you find another husband."

Frustrated, Salome threw an apple at him. Then she looked at her mother, who just laughed.

As their journey took them up into the hills, some of those with children began falling behind. When they came to an open patch of grass surrounded by trees, Ophellius rode up ahead to join Herod and those at the front of the convoy. "My lord..." he called, "We have been travelling all night. Many of the people have children. They need to rest and eat."

Herod glanced back at them, and looking around, nodded. "Very well. This is as good a place as any. Make camp. We will ride over the ridge and scout out the way ahead.

"Yes, my lord." Ophellius headed back and signaled the other guards and soldiers to bring the convoy to a halt and make camp.

"Commander!" a scout called to Joseph as Herod and the others headed up to the top of the ridge.

"What is it?"

"My spies have reported seeing Parthians searching the towns and villages."

"Are they looking for us?"

"Among other things," the scout reported.

When Joseph joined the others on the ridge, he rode up beside Herod and reported, "Scouts report that those Parthian dogs are moving throughout the land, plundering town after town. They're looking for us as well as gold and highborn women."

"The price Antigonus offered them, no doubt, in exchange for the throne," Herod murmured.

"Yes, well, from what he's hearing, many of the people want Antigonus out, and they want you to lead the war against him."

"We're already at war against him..." Herod murmured wearily. "Look at us...we're losing."

The sudden onset of a horse's hooves, beating the ground in a rapid gallop, drew their attention to the tree line. "Lord Herod!!" Ophellius called, emerging through the brush; his eyes filled with panic. "We're under attack!"

"Parthians?" Herod asked.

"No. Judeans!"

Herod and the others immediately followed him.

When they arrived back at the camp, it looked like a battlefield. Bodies—both their people and that of the enemy—lay scattered on the ground, covered in blood. Herod immediately joined the battle, cutting down several men within the first few seconds. "Where are the women and children?" he called to Ophellius as he hacked and slashed his way through the enemy line.

"In the wagons!" Ophellius pointed towards the hilltop where Pheroras was driving the cart containing the royal women and children, away from the battle. A group of soldiers were with him, protecting them.

"Go protect the royal family!" Herod ordered, riding his horse through a pair of rebel fighters, attacking from either side. Ophellius nodded and called Costobarus to join him as he headed off. Hippicus joined the archers on higher ground picking off enemy fighters, and Sohemus rode through the battlefield, smashing as many enemy skulls as he could. Joseph joined Herod, but he insisted, "Go protect our family!" Joseph nodded and rode off in the direction of the others.

Vehement supporters of King Antigonus, the rebel Jews, outnumbered Herod's army by thousands. They assumed attacking the governor while he was downtrodden and on the run, would have assured them victory; they were wrong. Little did they know, Herod had been leading men into battle since the age of 15 and governing since the age of 16. He may have been outnumbered and downtrodden, but he was a man bred in war.

Under his command, his men slaughtered hundreds of them. Realizing they were ill equipped to take him on, the enemy scattered and went scurrying back to their homes. Herod's men erupted into rousing cheers, but the victory was short lived.

"Lord Herod! Lord Herod!" From the way Ophellius was driving his stallion over the hill, and the dire expression on his face, Herod knew something terrible had happened.

"What is it?"

Barely bringing his horse to a halt, Ophellius called, "Come quickly!"

Herod rode off after him without hesitation.

When he arrived at the top of the hill, he saw an overturned wagon. Its canopy was mangled. A few feet away, a crowd was gathering around one of the camp tents. Herod pushed his way through. Their faces were a blur; their silence, damning. His senses heightened, Herod could hear the sound of his heart thumping in his chest as he drew closer. He saw Salome, Doris, Miriam, his brother and uncle kneeling in a circle, tears streaming down their faces. Suddenly, Herod became aware of their voices wailing and sobbing. His heart pounding, each step becoming harder; he looked past them. There, lying on a makeshift stretcher, covered in blood, dirt and bruises, was Cypros. She seemed near death. "MOTHER!!" His body suddenly weakening, Herod fell to his knees.

He took her hand and called to her, but she was unresponsive.

The physician looked at him and said gravely, "There is hope of her recovery...if she awakens." But the heavy sigh that followed, denoted his doubt that she would wake up.

Herod stepped away. Distraught, he stood looking around at them all: Princess Alexandra; the women and children sobbing; the men—many of them wounded, others lying dead on the hillside—and at the center of it all, his mother lying gravely wounded. His eyes filled with tears, Herod suddenly drew his sword and lifting it, plunged it towards his gut. Before the tip could pierce his armor, Sohemus, Hippicus and Joseph lunged at him, restraining his arms. "NO HEROD!!" they yelled.

"Let me go!!" he cried, trying to force the blade in. "I am to blame!"

"You are not to blame!" Joseph exclaimed, restraining him. "You are not the one who started this war!"

Seeing the commotion and what her brother was about to do, Salome marched over to him. She slapped him and shrieked, "What do you intend to do? Leave us...to be destroyed by your enemy! All who have followed you! Laid down their lives for you! Would you abandon us? Me! Your brothers!

Our mother! You would leave us to be sold into slavery or murdered!"

"Our mother lies dying!"

"She is not dead yet!" Salome hissed. The crowd grew silent. Salome looked across at Miriam and Doris. "And what of your wives, your son? What will become of them? You selfish man!!"

Herod turned his gaze to Miriam, and Doris clinging to his son. At the sight of the terror in their eyes, the sword slipped from his fingers and he began to sob. "Forgive me!"

As his friends released him, the women rushed into his arms, and the three of them sobbed, while the infant cried. The moment was dwarfed by the faint groans of Cypros stirring and the physician crying out, "She's awake! She's awake!"

Realizing he had almost ended his life for nothing, Herod closed his eyes and kissed Miriam and Doris on the forehead, then rushing to his mother's side, ordered everyone to leave.

Once everyone had left, Herod looked down at his mother and said, "I'm sorry, Mother." She smiled at him. He leaned down and kissed her forehead.

When he lifted his head again, Lucifer was crouched down across from him. He scowled sourly, "Do you think I would let you end your life before you have served your purpose?" He stood up. In an instant, he was behind Herod, while *Pride, Greed, Malice, Envy, Jealousy and Destroyer* appeared and encircled him. Lucifer grabbed Herod's head with one clawed hand as he produced a tarnished goblet with the other, which he held before the demons. Each one opened their mouths and spewed venom into the cup, while Lucifer looked down at Herod and snarled, "You are weak...sentimental! But NO MORE!" He pulled his head back and poured the vile of black venom down his throat, making him gag. As the last of it went down, Herod gasped for breath.

Suddenly opening his eyes, Herod sat up, gasping. He looked around. To his surprise, he was on his bed, alone in his tent. He couldn't recall how he had gotten there, or even when, but it was now morning. With beads of sweat running down his brow, he breathed a sigh of relief and lay back down. The vivid images still fresh in his mind, staring up at the canopy of his tent, he thought to himself, *what a strange and terrifying dream.* While he pondered its meaning, it dawned on him...something felt different.

14

KEEPERS OF HOPE

Pacorus cringed. He was overpowered by the smell of dried blood and bodily excrements splattered on musty straw and the cold stone floor. The sight of moldy bread on metal plates was enough turn his stomach, let alone the overwhelming stench of urine. He put his hand to his nose and looked for windows; there were none, only small openings in the rock-face to allow the flow of air. The main source of light came from torches flickering on the walls, and a shaft of sunlight beaming down through the winding stairwell.

Palace guards led the Prince and his bodyguards to a large cavern at the end of the hall. It was carved out of the rock foundation beneath the barracks. He passed by a handful of prisoners who were peering out of their cells, moaning and begging to be set free. Their incessant pleads began to drown out Antigonus' ranting until a burly general, named Hiam, yelled, "Quiet!!"

Prince Pacorus sat down in the prison guard's chair. He was relieved when a pretty servant girl named Sofera—who worked in the prison—came with a gold cup and a pitcher of wine. Perhaps getting drunk would help dull his other senses. With his cup full, the prince shooed away the servant and then stared at the royal prisoners through the iron bars of their cell. He wanted to hear what was being said.

"Where is Herod?" Antigonus raged. "Where did he hide the gold?"

"How are we to know? You have held us prisoner for days!" Hyrcanus grumbled. He was chained to the walls at opposite ends of the large cell.

Ignoring his uncle, Antigonus scowled at Phasael, "WHERE IS HE!!"

Glaring at the prince defiantly, Phasael answered, "Where you will never find him!"

King Antigonus balled his fist and pounded viscously on the governor's face until blood poured from his mouth, and Antigonus' fist hurt. He had been questioning them for hours, to no avail. Frustrated, he walked away to confer with

Prince Pacorus. As they argued, Sofera looked at Phasael slumped against the wall spitting out blood, and Hyrcanus, also battered and bruised. While the others were occupied, she poured out a cup of water and quietly headed to the cell. She put the cup to Hyrcanus' lips and let him drink. "Thank you," he whispered then glanced at Phasael.

After checking that King Antigonus and the prince were still distracted, Sofera quietly went over to Phasael. She lifted his chin and using the hem of her garment, wiped the blood from his mouth then put the cup to his lips. A hand suddenly grabbed her by the hair and slammed her into the wall, knocking her and the cup to the ground, before Phasael could take a sip. "What do you think you're doing?" Antigonus railed.

"My lord, it is customary to give the prisoners water and bread," she explained, rubbing the side of her face that hit the wall. She could feel her lip and cheekbone swelling, and the taste of blood was on her tongue.

"Do you not see I am interrogating the prisoners! I ought to chain you up with them! You give them nothing, unless I say so!"

"Yes, my lord," she answered, trembling.

"Get out!"

Her hands shaking, Sofera picked up the cup and hurriedly left the cell, glancing back at the prisoners.

"Water and bread..." Antigonus murmured. Infuriated, he looked at the guards and ordered, "You make sure they get nothing! Not even water! Let them starve!" He glared at Phasael and threatened, "Perhaps hunger will loosen your tongues!"

****

Herod and his men remained entrenched on the hillside until his mother was well enough to travel, then they continued on to Idumea. Meantime, their numbers continued to grow. People, angered by Antigonus' Parthian alliance, and many who had fallen victim to their rampage as they searched for highborn women and gold, flocked to Herod's side. They may not have approved of the Half-Jew, but life under him and King Hyrcanus was far better than what they were being subjected to under the rule of the usurper— Antigonus.

By the time they reached the Idumean border, their numbers were so vast it had become impossible to feed them. After meeting with Seth, and discussing the matter with his council, Herod gathered the people in a rocky valley and stood on a large boulder. "Many of you have journeyed from far to join our ranks," he announced. "You see that life under the tyranny of our enemy...is no life at all." His voice bounced off the surrounding rocks, making him audible to all. "I am grateful for your support, but most of you are not soldiers. You have come with your wives, your children, your slaves and your belongings. The battlefield is no place for them. Our numbers are great, but our provisions are low. If we remain as we are, the enemy will come and they will slaughter many." Some of the people began to protest, but Herod calmed them down and continued. "Hear me out. If we are to take back Jerusalem, then we need soldiers! Far greater in number than what we have now! Men who can fight and defeat our enemy! I will gather that army! But while I do, I need you to go."

"Go where!" one of them shouted, riling up the others.

Calming them, Herod continued, "Gather all those who want these Parthian dogs to leave of our land! Root out our enemy! Stop them from pillaging our land! My men will join you and fortify our strongholds, and together, we will begin to take back what is ours!"

The people began to cheer. Herod gestured to Seth, "My brother, Seth, will give you gold and provisions for your journey. Take it and go. I give you my solemn word, that when I return, I will not stop until every last Parthian is dead or has been driven from our land with their tails between their legs! And the throne of Judea is back where it belongs!"

To his surprise, the people not only began to cheer, but also chant his name. Herod looked on them. It was the first time he could remember, standing before such a vast Jewish crowd and not being the object of their scorn or hatred. The feeling was exhilarating. He had become the Keeper of their Hope. With the venom of pride beginning to seep into his heart, the demon—Pride, appeared on the top of a rock, looking down on him with his black eyes. Unaware of what was beginning to take shape in his heart, Herod lifted his head and smiled to himself.

Seth supervised the distribution of a good portion of Herod's wealth to the people, along with water and provisions for their journey, which he and his men had brought from the Idumean capital. Herod watched them leave. He had kept 800 men with him to serve as an armed escort, and sent the rest with the crowds as they scattered across the land. Be it soldier or mercenary, each man was tasked with leading the revolt against

Antigonus, and securing Herod's strongholds until his return.

After a brief visit to the Idumean capital to secure the rest of his wealth, Herod and his family left to take refuge in his fortress, called Masada.

****

As the days passed, the questioning continued while King Antigonus endeavoured to starve his prisoners in an attempt to make them talk. Guards were posted outside the cell, around the clock, but each night, Sofera waited until Antigonus and Prince Pacorus had left, and then asked the guards if she could clean the cell. It took but a reminder of how offensive the new king and his Parthian ally found the smell of the prison, for the guards to agree to allow her in.

In the brief moments she was in there cleaning the floor, as she neared the prisoners, she pulled out a small piece of cloth from under her garment. Without a word, she slid it by their bruised hands.

After she left and the guards started nodding off, Hyrcanus and Phasael opened the cloths, finding inside a small piece of bread and a handful of grapes and raisin cakes. In the darkness, they turned their heads to the wall and ate quietly and carefully, savoring every morsel. It wasn't much, but it was the best she could do without getting caught. And in the face of their misery, it was enough to strengthen their resolve and keep hope alive.

****

"So, tell me, Nephew..." Joseph asked as he rode beside Herod, up the narrow path leading to a mountainous plateau upon which Masada was built, "Where do you intend to find this vast army of yours? And more importantly, how do you plan to pay for it, seeing that you left the greater part of your treasure in Idumea?"

"You worry too much, Uncle," Herod answered smugly. "We cannot carry that amount of gold around with us. I will not allow it to fall into the hands of that Parthian scum."

"So, then what is your plan?"

"My priority is to get Phasael. He is of no real value to them."

"Except to use as bait in order to trap you," Joseph speculated.

"Antigonus wants me dead, but the Parthians only care about gold," Herod explained. "I will go to the king of Arabia and ask him for money to ransom back my brother, and pay for an army to take back Jerusalem."

"King Malchus?" Joseph snorted, "That old fart! He holds onto money tighter than a drunk holds onto his wine cup."

"He owes me. I have come to his aid on many occasion, and helped him defeat his enemies," Herod remarked.

"Do you know that many years ago, your father entrusted him with a chest of gold."

"He did?"

Joseph nodded. "For safe keeping, but when your father was murdered, the gold was forgotten about."

"So, by right, it is mine."

"Good luck in prying it from his chubby hands," Joseph chuckled.

"It is not I who will need it, but you."

"What?"

"I am sending you ahead of me."

"What! Why?"

Herod pulled to a halt. "I don't believe Phasael has much time. I do not have days to negotiate with him over food and wine. You will work out the terms of our agreement. Once things are settled here, we meet in a day or so at the Siq passage, en route to Rome."

"You're not stopping to see the king?"

"No time," Herod replied. "Once we have the money, you will go and offer that Parthian dog 300 talents of gold, and get my brother back, while I go and find an army to destroy them."

Before Joseph could protest, Herod raised his hand and signaled the others, shouting, "Hold!! We're here!"

15

ONE MORE THING

Out in the middle of the wilderness, and strategically built atop of a high plateau, this formidable fortress was an impressive feat of genius. Designed by Herod, it was accessible only by three narrow winding roads leading up to fortified gates. For those unfamiliar with the terrain, it was treacherous, surrounded by jagged cliffs and sheer drops on almost every side.

Behind its 13' high wall—erected around the entire circumference of the plateau—Herod had built storehouses, barracks, guard towers, baths and cisterns to catch rainwater. Its most impressive feature, however, was found at the furthest point on a narrow peak where Herod had built a beautiful 3-tiered palace. It was virtually impenetrable, and perhaps the only safe place in the kingdom to keep his family.

****

As fate would have it, a man named Zahid, happened to be passing through the area. He spotted Herod and his troops on their way up the narrow pathways, and hid himself among the rocks in the valley, watching as they entered Masada.

****

Having a good night's rest, after the long and weary journey, Herod sent his uncle Joseph off to Petra with a handful of men early the next morning. He also sent a messenger to Rome with a letter for Mark Anthony.

Members of Herod's family and the royal family, along with their servants, settled down in the upper tiers of the palace. Herod, however, allowed his close friends and relatives to take up residence in the lower tiers, as well as some of the guest and storehouses.

While the troops acclimated to the barracks, Herod and his brothers inspected the fortress. It was paramount they ensured there was enough food and supplies to last for some time. They found plenty of food and wine, but the cisterns were only half full and in need of repairs. Being quite skilled with his hands, and sharing his brother's creative streak, Pheroras assessed the damage and assured them, "I can have them repaired in no time. Don't worry brother…a good rainfall and we'll have them filled back up." With an optimistic smile, he beckoned some of the servants to help with repairs.

After spending the day, familiarizing Seth and his other commanders with the fortress: both its strengths and weaknesses, its weapons and supplies; at the end of the day, Herod sat down inside the palace at a very long and large oak table. He looked across at his mother and squeezed her hand. "You look well."

"I am fine, Herod," she replied with a reassuring smile. He looked to his right where Miriam was seated, then at the rest of the family seated around the table along with Hippicus, Sohemus, a few of his commanders—including Costobarus, and a handful of his most loyal nobles who had remained with them.

This was the first meal they had shared together with some sense of normalcy, since they had been forced to flee Jerusalem. Miriam looked at him and smiled, then bowed her head as he blessed their meal. When he was finished, the family began to eat. Miriam reached over to the platter of carved lamb, but as she reached for a particular piece, Doris, sitting across from her, quickly snatched it up. Miriam looked at her. Brandishing a spiteful glare, Doris took a bite and then dropped the rest on the floor for the dogs. She licked her fingers with a smug smirk until she noticed Herod. He watched one of the dogs walk off with the piece of meat, then looked back at Doris with a cold stare. Her smile fading, Doris lowered her gaze to her son.

Herod turned his attention to the rest of the family. With quiet resolve, he announced, "I am going to Rome." All the chatter stopped. The room grew silent, save the sound of the dogs licking the crumbs off the floor.

"Why?" asked Doris.

After swallowing a mouthful of wine, he answered, "Antigonus has a Parthian army at his disposal. The only way to defeat him is with a Roman army. If I can convince the Senate that he poses a threat to any peaceful rule over the Jews, they will give me a Roman army; I can finally crush this rebellion once and for all."

"So now you intend to drag us to Rome?" Doris snapped reproachfully, holding her son on her lap.

"No," Herod replied. 'I will take Sohemus, Hippicus and 100 men with me. The rest will remain here under Seth's command, to protect all of you."

"Herod..." Cypros started to protest, but he cut her off.

"Mother…the decision is made. I will not put any more of you in danger."

"And what of Phasael?" she asked.

"And my father?" added Alexandra.

Herod glanced at Hippicus and then replied, "Joseph has already left Petra to retrieve my father's gold. We will use it to ransom them back, and pay for the Roman army. I have sent a letter to Rome to inform Mark Anthony of my arrival, and I have requested reinforcements to protect all of you until I return." Herod shifted his gaze to Alexandra and added, "There's one more thing I will need…the boy."

Alexandra looked up at him. "What boy?"
Herod looked at the young prince.
"Who, Aris? What do you want with my son, lord Herod?" she hissed.
"I intend to have the Senate declare him king."
"King!" she scowled.
"Yes, or do you not wish it?"
"I wish it!" Aris responded, anxiously.
"Quiet Aris!" Alexandra stared at her son wide-eyed, and then looked back at Herod. "My father is king!"
"Your father is the prisoner of a man who wants him dead!" Herod replied, raising his voice.

"For all we know, he may already be dead! Our only guarantee of reclaiming the throne is to have Rome declare the boy, king!"

"He's right," Hippicus agreed. "If King Hyrcanus does not return, another is needed to take his place."

"Prince Aris is next in line for the throne, my lady," Ophellius stated.

"I don't care! He's my son, and the only heir to the throne of Jerusalem! He's not leaving my side!"

Glaring at her, Herod stood up, leaned forward and said sternly, "I was not asking."

Bold and defiant, Alexandra stood up and scowled at him, "Well, I'm telling you...you are not taking my son anywhere without me. If he goes to Rome, so do I!"

"If my mother goes, I go," said Miriam.

"If she going, I going!" snapped Doris, afraid that if she allowed her husband alone with his bride to be, she might lose him altogether.

"ENOUGH!!" shouted Herod. "The women stay here!"

Alexandra stabbed her knife into the table. Glaring at Herod, she snarled, "You have my only daughter! Aris is just a boy and he is all I have left! I will die, before I allow anyone to take him from me!"

After exchanging an icy glare, Herod looked around the table, and then murmured, "Fine. The boy stays." He sat down and resumed his meal, announcing, "I will have the Senate declare him king and crown him on my return."

"Then I will remain at the prince's side until you return, my lord," Ophellius announced, breaking the awkward silence.

"I too will stay, my lord," Costobarus announced, exchanging a quick look with Salome. "If the enemy attacks, I am sure Commander Seth could use all the help he can get."

Herod nodded in agreement. "Very well. Now, finish your meals. We leave at first light."

16

SOFERA

Antigonus stood inside the cell, staring at the prisoners. Prince Pacorus sat outside, holding a cloth over his nose, watching him impatiently. "How much longer must we endure this?" Pacorus growled, removing the cloth. "You have starved and beaten them for days and still they have given you nothing!" Annoyed, he railed, "The stench down here is intolerable! And I grow tired of these games! You make them talk or I am will order my men to murder all your priests! Starting with that pompous High Priest! And if that fails…" With a cold, glassy stare, he threatened, "I am going to start removing fingers…"

Antigonus looked at King Hyrcanus with a sneer on his face, imaging the Parthian prince cutting off his fingers, and his delight at hearing his uncle's harrowing screams. His smile broadened until Pacorus—staring directly at the usurper—added, "Namely, yours."

King Antigonus and his guards stared at the brazen prince, wide-eyed. "You dare to threaten me in my own palace?" he asked as his guards rested their hands on their weapons.

"Do not forget who put you in this palace, or that it was I who captured your king, and that my troops now keep your enemy at bay," Pacorus responded in an icy tone. "I assure you King, you do not wish to make an enemy of me. For I will march my men over to Herod and hand him your kingdom!" His bodyguards drew their weapons, as did Antigonus'.

"You wouldn't!"

"Try me." After a moment of awkward silence, Prince Pacorus signaled his guards to stand down. "Now, I can order my men to slaughter yours and turn Judea back over to its rightful king, or you can get me some answers!" Prince Pacorus turned his gaze back to the prisoners.

Antigonus signaled his guards to stand down. Glancing at his hands, and desperate for answers, Antigonus turned to the prisoners and started to draw a dagger from his belt. He hoped the threat would be enough to rattle their nerves.

"Antigonus!" Hyrcanus pleaded. "Do not do this! We came to you in good will, seeking peace."

"Then you are fools!" he snarled.

"Please, Nephew! We are blood, there is no need for this violence!"

"No need!" Antigonus skulked towards his uncle, snarling, "You caused this civil war! You took the throne and the priesthood! Forced my father…"

"It was your father who started this war! Not I!"

"You drove him to it! With your selfishness and greed! And now my father and brother are dead!!"

"I tried to make peace."

"Peace! 30 years of bloodshed! When all you had to do was choose…King or High Priest! Well, you will never have to make that choice again! HOLD HIM DOWN!" A pair of guards restrained Hyrcanus' arms, while a third grabbed him by the hair and pulled back his head so he couldn't move. Antigonus drew the dagger and grabbed his uncle's ear. Hyrcanus shrieked as he sliced off his right ear, and then his left, throwing them to the ground, covered in blood. Screaming in agony and horrified, as the guard released him, Hyrcanus scurried back against the wall. Wailing, he held his hands over the wounds as blood gushed through his fingers. "Now, I've stripped you of both the throne and the priesthood!" his nephew taunted.

Prince Pacorus looked at Hiam for an explanation. "I don't understand, what does he mean?"

The burly guard leaned down and replied quietly, "According to Jewish law...none who are maimed or blemished can serve in the priesthood. Hyrcanus can never be High Priest again."

Leaving his uncle whimpering on the ground, Antigonus looked over at the governor. "Now...Phasael, tell me where to find Herod and the gold, and I will make your death quick."

Phasael smirked, "Even if I knew...I would never tell you!"

Antigonus put up his dagger and walked over to a wall from which hideous weapons were hanging: hooks, clamps, knives and several other tools of torture. The king ran his fingers from one weapon to the next until he came across a cat-o-nine. He took it down and looked it over. Used to scourge, it had nine whips instead of one. Each whip had a metal prong on the end, designed to tear flesh from bone. He turned to the governor and grimaced, "I assure you, before I am done, you will tell me everything!"

"No!" Phasael snarled, clambering to his feet. "This day, I die knowing my brother will live to avenge me!" He suddenly turned to the wall and slammed his head against the protruding rocks.

"NOOO!!" The shrill of voices, from the king to the guards, echoed throughout the prison. Sofera screamed, and Prince Pacorus almost jumped out of his skin, knocking over his chair as he watched Phasael's body slump to the ground— blood pouring down his face.

The weapon fell from Antigonus' fingers. Mortified, he looked at Prince Pacorus. The prince scowled, "YOU FOOL!"

Antigonus shifted his gaze back to Phasael and screamed at the guards and servants, "Don't just stand there! Do something!! Do not let him die!"

One of the guards shoved Sofera towards him, while another unlocked his chain and rested his head down gently. Sofera tore the hem from her garment and pressed it against the wound. "Quickly..." she said, trembling, "fetch me water!"

As one guard hurried off to get water, the others stood back gawking at him. Sofera tried to keep pressure on the gaping wound in his cracked skull, but the governor, half conscious, groaned weakly, "Please...let me die."

Sofera glanced over her shoulder. The king and Prince Pacorus were engaged in a bitter argument, each laying blame on the other. She looked down at Phasael and carefully pulled out a small vial of ointment from a pouch. As she leaned down, she poured the black ointment into the wound, and with a gentle smile, whispered in his ear, "Your brother escaped with the royal family and your kin. They are safe." Phasael looked up and weakly smiled.

By the time the guard returned with the water, the governor wasn't moving. Hiam pushed Sofera out of the way. Feeling for his breath, he reported, "He's dead."

Greatly annoyed, Prince Pacorus grabbed Antigonus and snarled, "See what you have done! Now, we will never find out where Herod hid the gold!" Both the king and the prince's guards put their hands on their weapons, ready to draw them at a moment's notice, but the prince released him.

"There must be others who know!" Antigonus said fearfully, afraid of what the angry prince might do. "I will find them!"

"Oh, and how is that?" Pacorus grumbled. With all the commotion, Sofera pushed the vial back into her garment and quietly slipped out of their presence. Moments after she left, glancing down at Phasael's body, Hiam noticed a black substance in the gaping wound. "My lords..." he called, "You should see this."

When the prince and the king came over, they knelt and examined it. It was sticky and bore a strange odor. "What is it?" Pacorus asked.

Antigonus smelt it. Recognizing the substance, he scowled, "Rat Poison." He immediately looked around and asked, "Where's the servant girl?" The guards looked around, she was nowhere to be found. He stood up and barked, "FIND HER!"

Holding his hand over his severed ears, Hyrcanus began to laugh. The prince and the king looked at him. "What about this one?" Prince Pacorus asked. "What is to be done with him? Killing him will surely incite a riot."

Antigonus walked towards his uncle and snarled, "Kill him? Why should I make him a martyr? I am not going to kill him…"

"Then what do you intend to do with him?" the prince asked.

With a sinister grimace, Antigonus leaned down and snarled in his uncle's face, "I'm going to let you rot in a Babylonian dungeon!" Antigonus stood up and ordered, "Seal his wounds! And get him ready to travel!" As he and the prince walked out, Hyrcanus' screams once again echoed throughout the dungeon as guards held him down while Hiam took a searing hot knife and pressed it against his wounds.

****

Managing to get out of the palace gate before guards sounded the alarm, Sofera threw a blue shawl over her head and blended into the passing crowds. While guards searched the palace grounds for her, she made her way through a nearby market until she came to a small group of merchants—men she knew had remained loyal to Hyrcanus. "I'm looking for Zoltan," she asked one of them. The man took her around the corner to a young, dark-skinned man. He was loading various garments and produce onto a cart to sell in Israel. "Zoltan."

"Sofera, what are you doing here?"

"I'm in trouble. I need your help," she desperately pleaded.

"My help? Woman, the city is under siege. What is it you think I can do for you?"

Moving in closer, she said quietly, "The guards are looking for me. I need you to take me to Governor Herod. I have news concerning his brother and the king."

Zoltan nodded in agreement. Looking around, he removed a couple of planks of wood from the side of his cart, revealing a small compartment. He removed several weapons from it—weapons he was smuggle out of the city. "Get in. And whatever happens, keep quiet."

After she climbed into the compartment, he covered it back and finished loading his cart. He then climbed on and drove it towards the city gate. When he got there, Antigonus' guards inspected the cart, but finding only garments and food, they allowed him to leave.

Once out of view, Zoltan brought the cart to a halt and opened the compartment. He pulled Sofera out. "Gather some food and blankets," he said, as he started unhitching the cart. When they were done, he climbed up onto the horse and pulled her up behind him. Wrapping her arms around his waist, she asked, "Where are we going?"

"I've heard rumors that Herod was last seen heading to Masada, so that is where we will go."

17

A KING'S RANSOM

After watching Herod say a tearful goodbye to his wives, sister and younger brothers, Cypros pulled him aside. "Herod..." she said, forcing a smile.

"What it is, Mother? You are not still worried about my journey?"

She looked up and caressed his face. "You are my son, I will always worry about you. But that is not it."

"Then what?"

Cypros lowered her gaze, wringing her scarf in her fingers. "Before you go to Rome and claim the throne for Prince Aris, there is something I must tell you; something I have never spoken of, until today...."

Alexandra was standing up on the wall, watching her son peering out over the arid landscape, when she noticed Herod and his mother glance up the prince, whilst talking quietly. Though she couldn't hear them, she could only conclude their conversation was about him.

"Mother!"

"Yes, my son."

"When lord Herod returns, will I be king?"

Alexandra smiled. "Yes. He is going to return with a Roman army and take back the kingdom, then declare you king."

"Good. I have many plans for Jerusalem."

She smiled and brushed her hand through his curly hair. "I am sure you do." She pulled him in front of her, wrapping her arms around his shoulders as she turned her attention back to Herod. He kissed his mother, before climbing onto his horse and joining his troops. There was something unsettling about the way he and Cypros looked at her and her son as he rode off through the gates.

****

In Jerusalem, Itiel—who was now serving as King Antigonus' butler—led a small group of visitors into the throne room, escorted by guards. "My king, you have visitors," he announced, bowing and stepping aside.

A rabbi, dressed in a prominent white robe and shawl over a dark woolen garment, came before the king, accompanied by four well-dressed, finely groomed young men. "King Antigonus...do you remember me?" the rabbi asked.

Antigonus smiled, "Of course, Rabbi Babas. How could I forget my father's favorite cousin? You are one of our most powerful allies."

"I supported your father's claim to rule, and I am saddened to hear of his demise and that of your brother, Alexander. I have come to pledge you my support as our king and rightful heir to the throne."

The king stepped down from his throne and greeted his cousin warmly. "I am most appreciative of your support, Rabbi. Men like you are the cornerstones upon which Jerusalem's greatness is built." He turned his attention to the four young men accompanying him. "And who are these?"

"My sons: Nahor, Zachiah, Malachi and Dani. All of them are men of great wealth and highly revered. They hold great power and influence among the people."

"As do you, Father," Malachi noted.

"Yes, but I am too old to rally the people. You, my son, are not." He smiled, "Malachi, my youngest, he is always eager to please." Babas looked around at all the nobles, servants and guards in the throne room; too many ears for his comfort. He gestured to the window. "Is that a new papaya tree? It has been many years since I have seen the gardens."

Realizing that the Rabbi was seeking privacy, King Antigonus invited him to take a stroll through the royal gardens.

The two walked along the path beneath the shade of the palm trees with the king's guardsmen walking a few paces behind, and Babas' sons following behind them. "I always believed the queen's appointment of your uncle to the throne was a mistake," Babas said quietly. "That crown belonged on your father's head, not your uncle's. He has always lacked the strength to rule..."

"You mean backbone," King Antigonus murmured. "My uncle is a spineless puppet of those mongrels who should be our slaves."

"I could not agree more. That is why I am here, to offer you the full support of my house. None of us wishes to see Hyrcanus and the Half-Jew's return to power—the way they suckle at the teat of Rome, it's shameful. For many years, my sons and I have rallied the people against them. As a matter of fact, the very day Hyrcanus returned to power, two of my sons witnessed their friend, Simon, slaughtered right outside the palace gates by one of Herod's brutes. He could have just had him arrested, but instead he slaughtered him like a dog, just to drive fear into his enemies."

"The man is an animal," Antigonus remarked. "Unfit to rule."

"Yes, well, you will be pleased to know, my sons and I have been working tirelessly, along with many of the ruling council, to bring them down. We have financed and organized protests; attacks on the palace, and the ambush of their supplies. We have also destroyed their granaries, and supplied their enemies with weapons..."

"I dare say...my own campaign would have suffered greatly, if not for your help."

"Well, my sons are already rallying the people to support you as king. They will ensure that you have the loyalty and support of all the great houses of Jerusalem."

"Does that support include their wealth?"

"Whatever you need, you shall have our backing."

Shrewd like his father, his hands cupped behind his back as they strolled along the path, King Antigonus asked, "While I am glad for the support, I am no fool, cousin. The rich do not stay rich by offering their wealth to others, without a price. What is it yours?"

His hands folded inside his bell sleeves, Babas looked at him through the corner of his eye. "Well, added protection, for one," he answered. "We have wealth; you have a powerful army. I am sure you can spare two thousand men to protect the more prominent houses in the city, in the event of unrest."

"And two?" Antigonus asked.

Babas smiled to himself and answered, "Taxes. Herod had Hyrcanus lay heavy taxes on us in order to satisfy Rome's greed. I trust you will find a more lenient way to deal with the matter."

"You mean levy the taxes on the poor and working class instead?"

"And in exchange, we shall ensure you have the support of both the people, and the ruling council. After all, one hand washes the other."

"Consider it done."

"My king!!" Itiel called, hurrying past the guards.

"Did I not give explicit orders, we were not to be disturbed?" Antigonus scowled.

"You did, my king...but I believe you will want to hear what this man has to say. He knows where to find Herod." Itiel turned around and gestured towards the palace doors. Zahid stepped out of the shadows.

18

THE JOURNEY

Upon arriving at Masada and discovering that Herod had left for Petra, Zoltan and Sofera immediately left with a fresh horse, supplies and a two-man escort, but not before informing his family of the tragedy that had occurred in the prison. As they left the fortress and the news spread, loud sobs were heard echoing through the valley—the weeping voices of his mother, sister and brothers, along with his wife and children.

****

"So...first, we get the gold from Petra?" Hippicus asked as they neared the Siq passage.

"Um hum," Herod replied, signaling his men to slow down.

"And you are sure King Malchus is willing to give it up?" Hippicus asked in a cynical tone.

Herod smiled to himself and replied, "He's family, of course he will."

****

"No," Joseph said, facing Herod at the entrance of the Siq passage.

"What do you mean 'No'?" Herod demanded, staring at the large Nabatean army situated at the mouth of the narrow sandstone canyon, leading to Petra's treasury.

"King Malchus said, 'No. You cannot have the gold." Joseph repeated.

"That's not possible. Did you talk to him directly?"

"They wouldn't even let me enter the city. We've been camped out here for three days, sending messages to the king."

"And he has not received you?"

"No."

"Why?"

Joseph shrugged and gestured towards the Nabatean vizier, "Ask him."

Herod turned his attention to vizier who was standing in a chariot at the head of the Nabatean army, blocking their passage into the city. "What do you mean, 'No'?" Herod demanded.

"The king said, 'No'. You may not enter the city, nor will he give you his gold."

Herod glared at him, taken aback. "It is my father's gold!! Not his!"

"It makes no difference whose gold it is, the Parthians have threatened to destroy our city if we help you in any way. Therefore, the gold stays here."

"Where is Malchus?" Herod scowled. Enraged, he roared. "MALCHUS! MALCHUS! I need that gold to ransom my brother! SHOW YOURSELF!!" At the echo of his voice bouncing off the towering sandstone walls, Nabatean soldiers emerged at the top of the winding canyon with arrows drawn. Those standing behind the vizier drew their swords and spears, ready to fight. Herod surveyed the many arrows trained on them and shouted, "Does the blood of your kin mean nothing to you!! How many times have you come to me for help! Have I ever turned you away? How many of my men have died fighting your wars! I have come to your aid, time and time again! And this is how you repay me!" YOU OVERSTUFFED PIG!!" Receiving no response from the king, who he knew—whether directly or by servant—was hearing the echo of his voice, Herod turned his cold, belligerent eyes back to the vizier and scowled, "You tell that sniffling coward, he will regret this!! I swear by the blood of my father! I WILL MAKE HIM PAY FOR THIS TREACHERY!!" With a foreboding glare, he tugged on his horse's reigns and turned away without another word.

They rode back through the canyon in silence. When they reached the other side, Sohemus and Hippicus looked at Herod. Sohemus asked gently, "Herod, what do we do now?"

Herod looked towards the desert and scowled, "We go to Egypt and get a ship."

"With what?"

"A promise." he snarled.

They continued their journey, camping in an old abandoned temple that night. As the sun began its descent over the mountains, casting a shadow across the stone pillars, and his men were talking among themselves, Herod stood inside his tent, mulling over the things his mother had told him before leaving Masada. His mind weighing heavily on Phasael, he stretched out his arms, while his armor bearer unbuckled his breastplate. His thoughts were suddenly interrupted when a ruckus started outside. Hippicus barged in. "What is it?" Herod asked, waving off the servant. Hippicus stared at him, deeply troubled. They had been friends long enough for Herod to know that look. Breathing a heavy sigh, the commander opened the flap and stepped aside. Zoltan entered, and gave way to Sofera. The two fell to their knees before him. "Where have you come from?" Herod asked, suddenly becoming aware of his rapid heartbeat.

"We bring news from Jerusalem, my lord," Zoltan answered. "This woman here, she worked in the prison where the king and Governor Phasael were being held."

Feeling his knees weakening, Herod sat down. "Rise. What news do you have of my brother and the king?"

Sofera stepped forward, her gaze lowered, she said. "My lord, the king is alive..." with a heavy sigh, and tears welling in her eyes, she added, "But your brother...is dead." A bewailing shriek bellowed from Herod's tent, echoing through the temple for several minutes.

"Tell me what has happened!" he growled, trembling with rage and grief.

Sofera knelt before him and explained all that had happened at the prison. "He begged me to let him die before Antigonus could torture him to death," she sobbed, showing him the vial of poison.

Herod rested his hand on her head. "You showed him kindness; I will not forget that." He looked at Zoltan and ordered, "Take her back to Masada."

"Yes, my lord."

Turning to Sofera, he said, "From now on, you will serve in the king's palace as handmaid to my betrothed, Princess Miriam."

"Thank you, my lord." As she got up and bowed, she reassured him, "Your brother died well: without pain and knowing that those he loves are safe, and that you will avenge him."

His eyes growing cold, Herod growled, "Of that, you can be assured."

"My lord," Zoltan said, stopping at the entrance as he and Sofera headed out, "This may not be the right time...but, it would be my honor to serve with your troops. I can fight...well."

"Then this is just the right time," Herod replied. "I will need men like you to help me take back this kingdom, and wipe out our enemies!" Lowering his gaze, Herod added, "And protect my family."

"Gladly, my lord."

"Help my brother Seth defend Masada. Tell him, I must go to Egypt, and from there, to Rome. I will send a messenger when we have crossed the Grecian sea."

"I will, my lord. We will leave right away." Zoltan left the tent and followed Sofera out. Joseph gave them and their escort food, water and fresh horses before sending them on their way.

Alone in his tent, his head buried in his hand, Herod continued to weep over the death of his older brother. Remembering what happened the last time he thought he had lost a loved one, Joseph, Hippicus and Sohemus stood at the entrance of his tent. "Do we need to watch him?" Joseph asked quietly.

"No, you do not." Herod growled, looking up at them. His bloodshot eyes, filled with rage, he got up and moving away from the table, scowled, "I should have killed that bastard! I should have hunted him down and ripped open his throat!" He turned and looked at his uncle and his commanders. "I will no longer seek to take my life. I will avenge my brother with the blood of our enemy!! And I swear upon his blood, I will show them no mercy! No lenience to their kin. I will wipe out all who oppose me! None shall escape my wrath, ever again!"

Seated in his chair with his feet up on the table, Lucifer leaned back, and with a smile of satisfaction, remarked smugly, "Now that, is more like it!"

19

WIVES

Being blessed with a full moon and a clear sky, Zoltan and Sofera arrived back at the gates of Masada just before sunrise, after riding through the night. Seth welcomed them in and offered them food and a place to rest.

Residing in the upper tier of the three-tiered palace, and stirred by the chill of the morning air, Miriam rolled over and opened her eyes. The room looked strange and unfamiliar, then she remembered that she was no longer at the palace. She rolled back the covers and stepped down onto the cold mosaic floor, sweeping her curls from her face. Shivering, she drew a shawl over her shoulders and walked out to the crescent-shaped terrace.

The sun was just peaking over the horizon, but the sky was ablaze with color. Vibrant hues of yellow, pink and cerulean blue infused the sunrise with an extraordinary splendor. It was contrasted only by the dark silhouettes of the surrounding mountain range, stretching for miles. Ancient and magnificent, they rose from the desert in matchless grandeur, while shimmers of light danced across the silky waters of the Dead Sea. She had never seen such arid beauty from her palace in Jerusalem, or been in such awe of God's majestic creations. Despite all the turmoil they had faced, here—perched above the landscape— she was never more at peace. "You should be careful you don't fall," Doris said, startling her.

"I didn't know you were up..." she gasped.

The palace wasn't just built on the plateau; it was hewn into the rock-face. Doris strolled past Miriam to the outer pillars and gazed over the edge. Below them was the bathhouses, and beyond that, a treacherous sheer drop hundreds of feet. "A long way down." she muttered, "I doubt you would survive." She turned to head back inside, throwing an icy glance in the direction of the princess.

"Have I wronged you?" Miriam asked.

Doris halted and eyed her with a cold stare. "You? Who has stolen my husband, ask if you have wronged me?"

"It was not I who asked for him...he asked for me."

"Well, of course he did, after you flaunted yourself before him like a common harlot," Doris scowled, glaring at her.

Mouth wide open, Miriam gawked at her in disbelief. "How dare y...!"

The sudden blast of a ram's horn sounded, waking everyone. At the sound of her son crying, Doris ran inside, while Miriam ran around to the side and peered down. Troops were gathering in the valley below like a swarm of insects, making their way up the winding paths leading up to the fortress. She hurried back inside, meeting up with Alexandra and the young prince.

"Miriam, what is it?" asked Alexandra.

"It looks like soldiers!" she replied.

Pheroras came running inside and shouted, "We are under attack!" He ran back out.

"Stay here!" Ophellius called to the women. He ordered the guards outside not to allow the enemy through. Then he locked the doors and shouted at the guards inside, "We protect the royal family with our lives!"

Doris came back out, cradling her son. "Is it Antigonus?" she inquired desperately.

Miriam stared at her for a moment. In the face of danger, with all her pomposity stripped away, she was just another frightened mother, clutching her infant to her chest. She above all had reason to fear, knowing that if Antigonus managed to breech their defense, he would take her beloved son, whom she paraded about like a trophy, and make her watch as he threw him off the ridge, before throwing her and Herod's mother, sister and brothers off as well. Being of royal blood, Miriam and her mother would not face the same fate; they were more valuable as prisoners, but there was no telling what he would do to Prince Aris. She finally answered, "I am not sure."

20

Port of alexandria

King Malchus—normally jovial, and whose every thought centered on sumptuous delights—seemed somewhat devoid of his appetite after news of Phasael's demise reached his palace. Upon discovering the king's lavish table untouched, the vizier asked, "Is something the matter, my lord?"

King Malchus, who was seated on his throne, staring at the chest of gold on the floor before him, shifted his gaze and confided with a heavy sigh, "I believe I may have made a mistake."

"How so, my lord?"

"Herod wanted this gold to ransom his brother. My spies inform me his brother is dead, and now Herod is on his way to Rome to gather an army."

"An army to defeat the Parthians," the vizier observantly reminded him.

King Malchus looked at him and fearfully remarked, "And when he has defeated them, he will turn his wrath on me! You heard his threats...you don't know him as I do...he will not forget," Malchus mumbled, nervously biting his nails. "I should have given him the gold."

Watching the king, the vizier asked, "Might I ask, my lord...is it too late?"

King Malchus looked at him. "What did you say?"

"Is it too late to give him the gold? It will not bring back his brother, but...it may help to appease his anger."

The king's eyes lit up. "That is an excellent idea!" Servants hurriedly came to help him up as he clambered to his feet and ordered, "Prepare my chariot! And bring the gold! And Vizier...find out where Herod is now!"

"As you wish, my lord."

****

Leaving behind the noisy port, crowded with merchants and fishermen, and engulfed with the smells of fish and exotic spices, Herod and his men left the port of Alexandria on a Greek ship bound for Rome. With most of his men below deck, and now only the serge of the waves breaking across the bow, Herod turned his eyes towards a large chest he had acquired from Queen Cleopatra on the promise of prime Judean land. Filled with 1,000 talents of gold, he had two armed men guarding it at all times, and several others standing guard around them. As the ship sailed out into open waters, Hippicus heard a voice being carried on the wind. He looked towards the port where the overly dressed figure of a short, plumb man on a white and gold chariot was waving profusely. The man, surrounded by several guards, was calling out the name, "HEROD!! HEROD!!"

"Herod!" Hippicus called. As the governor approached, steadying himself against the rocking of the ship, Hippicus pointed to the port. "They're calling your name."

"That looks like Malchus," Joseph inquisitively exclaimed.

"What does he want?" Herod grumbled.

Hippicus pointed as Malchus lifted a fur pelt on his chariot, showing them a large chest. "Looks like he brought your gold. Should I order the captain to turn back?"

"No," Herod growled. "When I return from Rome with an army, I will take both my gold and his throne."

21

Masada

While Herod made his way across the Mediterranean Sea, battling through raging storms and violent winds, King Antigonus was leading an army of thousands of enemy soldiers against the fortress. At the head of them were two-dozen men with ropes attempting to pull a battering ram up one of the narrow winding paths, while three-dozen more pushed it from the sides and behind, trying to steady it. Hundreds of others were attempting to scale the jagged mountain.

Too large and clumsy for the narrow winding road, as they veered around a narrow bend, the ram toppled over, crushing those beneath it, and dragging off many of those on the ropes as it plummeted into the valley below and smashed into pieces.

Watching the disaster from the wall, Seth— who had divided the troops into three groups—

commanded his men to bombard those on the roads with burning rocks. Costobarus, commanding the archers on the wall, signaled them to fire on the troops further back. Sending Sofera to hide with the other servants, Zoltan joined Pheroras' men using rocks and arrows to pick off those scaling the mountain. Despite the bombardment, it didn't take the climbers long to realize that the climb was too treacherous and the rock-face too jagged to scale. Those who were not killed by Pheroras' men, one by one, slipped and fell to their deaths. Defeated, the enemy troops turned back, being taunted by jeers and laughter as they returned to their camp at the base of the plateau.

The next day, King Antigonus sent one of his captains back up the winding road with 2,000 men, this time on foot. The plan might have worked had the roads not been so narrow.

The first wave of men was extinguished by a slew of arrows—their numbers were too few to make an impact. Seth's soldiers picked them off with ease. The captain then decided brute force was needed, except the road wasn't wide enough for such numbers. As fiery boulders tumbled down towards them, King Antigonus and Prince

Pacorus sat in the shade of their tents listening to harrowing screams trail down the mountain as their soldiers plummeted off the path, dozens at a time. After listening to it for 20 minutes, Prince Pacorus had had enough. "Do you intend to fill this valley with the bones of my men? Order them to retreat!"

Humiliated, King Antigonus reluctantly ordered one of the guards, "Sound the horn! Have them retreat!" To the delight of those in the fortress, the enemy retreated.

"I suggest you come up with a better plan," The prince scolded.

Annoyed, Antigonus stood up and ranted sarcastically, "Well, let's see...we cannot use a battering ram, we cannot scale the mountain and we cannot breech the gates. So, what do you suggest I do?"

"I don't know! Think of something!" the prince growled, walking off.

Frustrated, Antigonus swept his hand across his table, knocking everything off.

****

A wildly tumultuous storm left Herod and his crew shipwrecked on the shores of Rhodes, off the coast of Greece. Though they had lost much of the ship's cargo and several crewmen, they somehow managed to save the gold in the part of the wreckage that made it to shore. When they were found by friends of his and brought to their city—much of which had been damaged by war—Herod agreed to have his men help with repairs, while the townspeople undertook building him a new ship.

****

There was a knock at Miriam's door. "Enter," she called.

One of her handmaids opened the door. Ophellius entered. "My lady, forgive the intrusion, but lord Herod has sent you a gift."

He stepped aside; Sofera entered and fell to her knees before the Princess. "My lady."

The princess looked at Ophellius and asked. "What is this? I have handmaidens."

"Lord Herod wanted her to serve you as a reward for her kindness to your grandfather and lord Phasael in the prison, before their death."

Miriam looked at her and smiled. "You are the one who came from Jerusalem."

"Yes, my lady," she answered, keeping her eyes lowered.

"What did you say your name was?"

"Sofera, my lady."

Miriam lifted her chin, and looking at her face, said, "Rise Sofera." Sofera rose. Miriam smiled at her and said warmly, "If my betrothed wishes you to serve me, then I welcome you into our household." She brushed Sofera's hair from her face. The maid looked her in the eyes. They were kind and gentle, and her tone warm—unlike those of the guards and warden she was used to in the dungeons. "You showed great kindness to Herod's brother and my grandfather, without a thought of your own life. Therefore, you shall be my chief handmaiden. You shall sleep in the palace and be at my side. And all the others will now take orders from you."

Overwhelmed with gratitude, Sofera bowed her head and kissed her hand, "Thank you, my lady!"

"First though, let's get you changed out of those old rags and do something with your hair." She beckoned the other maids who promptly ushered Sofera out.

When nightfall came and the royal household had all gone to sleep, Sofera went outside to get some air. As she stood out on the terrace looking up at the stars, she heard a, *"Psst!"* from up above. She went over to the steps at the left side of the palace. As she turned the corner, Zoltan startled her. "What are you doing out here?" she whispered, checking to see if anyone was around.

"Looking for you," he said quietly, glancing up the steps. "They posted me to guard the palace. I wanted to see how you were."

"I'm fine."

Zoltan stared at her. He suddenly realized the change in Sofera's appearance. Working in the dungeons, she was usually grungy: her clothes tattered, her hair a mess. She often carried a lingering smell of musky urine and a concoction of fragrant leaves, used in the water to clean the dungeon floors. When she noticed him staring, she asked, "What?"

He smiled. "Who would have guessed, beneath all that dirt and grime was a ravishing beauty." He sniffed her hair. It smelt like honey and perfumed oils. "You even smell different."

"Perfume," she said. Blushing, she grinned and looked him up and down. "And look at you, nothing like that ruffian from the market."

"Well, I'm a royal guard now."

"Um, all respectable...and handsome."

Realizing, he had taken notice of her words, Sofera changed the subject, bashfully showing him her new dress. "Real silk." She showed him how the soft layers of the cream silk garment twirled as she spun around. Almost losing her balance, Zoltan stretched out his hands and caught her as she fell into his arms. The two shared a moment, looking into each other's eyes, before Sofera quickly pulled away and lowered her gaze. "She made me chief handmaiden," she announced quietly.

"The princess?"

Sofera nodded. "Um hum."

"What is she like?"

Sofera looked towards the door and with a soft sigh, she smiled and answered, "She is kind and gentle...kinder than anyone I've known my whole life."

Zoltan stroked back her hair from her face. "I'm glad. It's not often life gives us what we deserve." He stared into her eyes. He had often looked at her before when she had come to the market to buy wares from him, but never like this, and she knew it. Out on the top of the plateau, in the middle of a war in the wilderness, under the clear night sky, something ignited between them.

Sofera smiled with him, but hearing the infant inside starting to fuss, she pulled away and whispered, "I have to go."

"I'll see you tomorrow."

He held onto her hand as she walked away. Before leaving though, she suddenly returned and kissed him on the cheek. "Thank you."

Surprised, he asked, "For what?"

"For risking your life and bringing me here."

"I brought you into a war."

"All we've ever known is war. At least here, we are among friends." She hurried off. Zoltan watched her until she went inside and closed the doors. He then headed back up the steps to his post, reporting that all was clear down below.

****

It had been several days since the usurper and his Parthian army had attacked Masada. King

Antigonus had spent days arguing over strategies of attack with Prince Pacorus and a handful of his commanders. None seemed to be able to come up with a viable solution that didn't involve losing half their army in the effort. Since most of the army was made up of Parthians, the prince rejected every suggestion. Early that morning while they argued, guards pushed open the flap of the king's tent. Zahid entered. "My lords! MY LORDS!" he shouted over their ranting.

Frustrated, King Antigonus looked at him and snapped, "What is it, Zahid?"

"A gift." Zahid gestured towards the entrance as a pair of guards dragged in a prisoner. He threw the man to the ground. "We caught him trying to sneak into Masada."

"Who is he?" the prince asked.

"From what we can gather, it seems he may have been trying to deliver a message."

King Antigonus peered down at the messenger and demanded, "What message?"

The servant clenched his lips together, and glared at him, determined not to talk. Zahid backhanded him. "Answer your king!"

"He is not my king!" the captive said defiantly. "I answer only to lord Herod and our true king—Hyrcanus."

King Antigonus drew his sword, but Prince Pacorus stayed his hand and ordered, "No," he stepped forward, "Summon Flox." A moment later, a large soldier entered. A permanent scowl on his bearded face, self-inflicted scares and burns all over his body—this Parthian ravished pain. "Flox...make this man talk."

A sinister grin curling on his lips, the large Parthian grunted, "Gladly." He grabbed the captive servant.

"Keep him alive!" Pacorus ordered as Flox dragged him out by the scruff of his neck. "He may be of use."

"What can he do that my men cannot?" Antigonus asked.

Taking a cup of wine from his cupbearer, the prince answered smugly, "You'll see."

They stripped the prisoner naked and tied him between a pair of wooden posts. Grimacing, Flox picked up a long knife and walked towards him. Harrowing screams followed, echoing throughout the valley.

Within minutes, guards pulled back the flap of the king's tent. Zahid returned and reported, "Herod is on his way to Rome. He intends to return with a Roman army to take back Judea. His servant was ordered to report that he has been delayed on his journey. Apparently, he became shipwrecked on the isle of Rhodes. A new ship is being built for him. When it is complete, he will resume his journey."

The allied leaders looked at one another. The news was not what they wanted to hear. "If he gets the Romans involved..." Pacorus murmured, "This is all over."

King Antigonus sat down dismayed. He looked at Zahid and asked, "If Herod is on his way to Rome...then who is in the fortress?"

Zahid replied, "His family."

Prince Pacorus inquired, "Are you sure?"

"I saw him arrive with them," Zahid assured him.

"He would not risk taking them to Rome," King Antigonus mused, strolling around his table. "Nor would he leave the fortress so well guarded if there was no-one of value inside." Antigonus looked at Prince Pacorus, "There's one thing that stands between his victory and ours…" He pointed to the fortress. "And they are within those walls. We capture Herod's family, and he will have no choice but to surrender Judea to me or watch them die."

"That's all well and good…" Pacorus replied. "but the question still remains…how do we take that fortress?"

While the allied leaders racked their brains for ideas, Zahid—looking out through the entrance of the tent—happened to observe several servant-girls going around the allied camp, giving water to the troops. "We are in the middle of the desert and it hasn't rained for months," he noted.

"So…" Antigonus grunted.

"As long as we remain here, they can neither leave the fortress, nor receive supplies." He looked at the two leaders and asked, "Why waste your men trying to attack when you can simply…starve them out?"

22

BATHWATER

"How are the supplies?" Seth asked as he and Costobarus walked the perimeter of the wall with Pheroras.

"We have food enough for a few more weeks, but...we are running low on water and wine. With our enemy camped out below, we have not been able to receive any new supplies," Pheroras replied.

Seth peered down at the camp below. "I get the feeling they are not going anywhere, anytime soon."

"They have not attacked in a while. Do you think they have given up?" Costobarus asked.

"Knowing Antigonus, more likely, they intend to starve us?" Seth muttered. "If they cannot breach our walls, perhaps they see this as their only choice."

"We have over 800 mouths to feed, including women and children," Pheroras noted. "Without new supplies or water..."

"I know..." Seth murmured with a concerned look. "We are not going to last more than a few weeks at most."

"That's if we last that long," Pheroras murmured.

"What do you mean?" asked Costobarus.

"We are in the middle of a desert on top of a ridge. Even if there is oil to cook meat and bake bread, we cannot survive without water." Pheroras answered.

"And men cannot stand and fight when they are dying of thirst," Seth added with a heavy sigh.

"Then we fight them now," Costobarus said aggressively.

Seth gestured to the sea of men below. They were like a swarm of insects. "They outnumber us at least 10 to 1. We step outside these gates and we would be slaughtered like sheep. Our only defense is that they cannot get in. As long as we remain here, we are safe."

Costobarus shifted his gaze to Seth, "But like you said...we can't last here forever. Not without water."

Surveying the fortress, Seth replied, "We just have to last until Herod returns with his army." After a moment of deliberation, breathing a heavy sigh, he commanded, "Costobarus, shorten the men's shifts. Make sure they conserve their energy." Then he looked at his brother and ordered, "Pheroras, ration the food and water. No more bathes or washing of garments. Give the women a small basin of water for the children. The rest is reserved for drinking."

"What about the dogs?" Pheroras asked, looking down at one of them as it started barking. "They serve as lookouts."

"I know." Rubbing his brow, Seth ordered, "but if it becomes necessary, slaughter them, and use them as meat, but keep the horses." The two men nodded and left.

****

As evening approached, Seth sat down in his quarters to eat a meager allotment of bread and dried meat with a quarter cup of water. There came a sudden pounding at his door. He barely opened it before Salome barged in, glaring at him with her cold, deep-set eyes. "Salome, what are you doing h…"

"Am I to understand that you ordered no more baths?"

"I did."

Narrowing her eyes, she demanded, "Why?"

"In case you have not noticed, we are at war. Our enemy surrounds us and they have cut off our supply route. No-one gets in or out."

"And?"

Seth rolled his eyes. "Our troops and servants number well over 700, all tasked with protecting our families. How long do you think they will last without food and water?"

"I don't care! I am not asking you to allow 700 to bathe…just me!"

"Come with me." Seth grabbed Salome by the arm and marched her out onto the wall. He pointed down to all the campfires throughout the valley. "Look! The enemy outnumbers us 10 to 1. Every day supplies and fresh water is brought to them. That means they can camp for as long as they want. Do you know why they have ceased their attacks?"

"No," she shrugged.

"Because they know, sooner or later we will run out of our supplies, and without receiving more...it's just a matter of time before we starve or die of thirst. And when that time comes...that water in the baths may be the only thing that stands between us and death!

"You expect us...me and your mother to drink bathwater!"

"If that's what it takes to stay alive."

"I will die before I drink bathwater!" she scowled.

"As you wish, Sister, but until Herod returns with reinforcements, my orders stand! No bathes! And all water and wine is to be rationed."

"You're rationing the wine!"

Realizing she clearly failed to grasp the seriousness of their situation, Seth put up his hand stopping her. Frustrated, he grumbled, "You want to lavish yourself with bathes and wine...then pray for rain."

****

It had taken weeks for a new three-decked ship to be built. But now, equipped with a vast supply of food, wine and water, Herod and his men finally set sail once again. Although they were met with calmer waters, the journey was far from over. They still had to sail around Greece and up the coast of Italy to reach their destination—Rome.

****

As the weeks passed, with no help in sight, the situation at Masada had become dire. The cisterns were now empty, as were most of the wine jars, leaving only what water remained in the baths; there wasn't much of that left either. Some had been used to water the horses, but all the other animals, including the dogs were gone. Guards, forced to stand in the baking sun for hours were already drinking water from the baths, but with little more than a mouthful for several hours, many were collapsing—first the wounded, then the old and poor in health. A few were even starting to die, as were some of the horses.

Barely having the strength to stand under the beating sun, Seth stood on the wall, staring down at the people and pondering what to do. It was bad enough to watch soldiers dying of thirst and exhaustion, but women and children; he didn't want their blood on his hands as well.

When Pheroras ordered Zoltan to check on the commander and bring him some water, Zoltan found him up on the wall. "Your brother asked me to check on you, Commander," he called, stepping up onto the wall. "He asked me to give you this." He handed him a wineskin; it was half-full of water.

"I told him not to do that," Seth murmured, taking it. "There are women and children down there, more in need of this than I."

"The troops take their orders from you," Zoltan said observantly. "How can they protect the royal family without their commander?"

Seth stared out over the western horizon, murmuring, "Herod should have been back by now. If he hasn't perished, then he has left us here to die."

"You don't really believe that?"

"I don't know what to believe anymore, but I can't watch all these people die, not this slow lingering death."

"What are we to do?" Zoltan enquired.

Seth rubbed his brow, "I don't..." In the corner of his eyes he suddenly saw Zoltan collapsing. He managed to grab him and help him down. "When was the last time you drank something?"

His mind a little hazy, Zoltan's thoughts ran on Sofera; he had given her most of his rations of water after discovering her on the verge of collapse. Although she had refused it at first, after watching her growing weaker by the day, he insisted. He knew rations were first allotted to those of royal and noble blood, then the guards, and finally the servants and horses. Although Princess Miriam had chosen to show her handmaidens extraordinary kindness, for her sake, they refused to take any of her water. Trying to clear his head, Zoltan mumbled, "I'm...not...I..."

Seth opened the wineskin and offered it to him. "Drink."

"No, Commander, I cannot take your water."

"Drink!" Seth insisted. "That's an order."

Zoltan reluctantly took the wineskin and put it to his lips. The feel of the liquid going down was so cool and refreshing, it was like extinguishing a fire on the inside of him. If he could, he would have to drank it all—even if it did taste bad. He stopped drinking and said, "Thank you." He handed the wineskin back to Seth, noticing a long scare on his left arm. "Where did you get that?" he asked.

Seth sat down beside him and looked at the scare. "On the battlefield of Jerusalem, some brute of a man almost took my arm off. You should have seen him, he was like a bear...." The two of them started to laugh wearily, when a soldier standing a few feet away suddenly fell backward. Seth tried to grab him, but he was too far. Before he knew it, the soldier hit the ground and his head smashed open on the rocks below. The moment turning somber, both men stared at him. Seth immediately ordered, "Get out of the sun. NOW!"

"Yes, Commander."

Inside the circular palace, perched atop of the forefront peninsula, about to pass out, Salome lifted a clay jar and put it to her mouth...it was empty. She threw it down and picked up a gold cup, managing to drain a few drops of wine—barely wetting her tongue. She slammed it down and went from one vessel to another; they were all empty. Frustrated, she hurled the last one at the wall, startling the others as it smashed. "Where is all the wine!"

"There is no more wine," Cypros answered, taking what little comfort she could in the cool waft of air being generated by the weary maid fanning her. She looked over at Alexandra as she put her wineskin to Prince Aris' mouth and allowed him to drink a few sips of water. "All that remains is the last of our water rations and a little bathwater."

"I will NOT drink water from the baths!!" Salome scowled.

"Oh, will you stop your whining!" Alexandra snapped. "First you complain because your brother refuses you a bath, and now you are refusing to drink the very water that could save your life! You should be grateful he had the wisdom to preserve it."

"Then why don't you drink it?" Salome scowled.

"Because I am royalty, and you are not," Alexandra snapped, growing tired of the argument. "But if there is nothing else..."

Just as Salome started to rebuttal, she was interrupted by a sudden thud: Cypros' maid collapsing from heat exhaustion. "Oh! By all the heavens!" Cypros murmured.

"She's exhausted, they all are," said Miriam, wearily looking around at the servants. With barely enough strength to move, she picked up her wineskin and went over to the maid.

As she passed her, Cypros pulled her arm and insisted, "The water is to be reserved for us and the guards."

Miriam glared at her and replied, "It's mine to give." She pulled her arm away, but as she lifted the maid's head, Doris came and snatched the wineskin from her hand.

"You will not waste our water on the servants and let my son die of thirst! If you want to give her water, then give her bathwater, or better yet...toss her off the terrace and save it for yourself!"

Miriam started to protest, but she relented when Doris put the wineskin to her son's lips. When she was done, she took a long gulp of water herself, glaring at the princess. Miriam just shook her head and picking up a cup, dipped it in a clay pitcher filled with bathwater and gave it to the maid to drink. Princess Alexandra, however, dragged herself up, stumbled over to Doris and snatched it away from her. "Know your place! She is royalty...you are not!" she hissed. "And the next time you speak to my daughter like that...you and I shall have words of a different sort!" She went back to her seat, putting Miriam's wineskin down beside her.

Salome, in the meantime, staggered out to the main doors and called, "Costobarus!" When he came to her, looking exhausted, she pleaded, "Would you please find me some water or better yet...wine?"

He took off his wineskin and offered it to her. "Here, the last of my wine." Salome smiled, and taking it from him, put it to her lips and drank deeply. "I mixed it with water from the baths," He added.

Horrified, she spat it out and shrieked, "YOU DID WHAT!! FOOL!!" She threw the wineskin at him and stumbled off.

Now almost empty, Costobarus growled, "That...was the last of my rations!"

23

PRAY FOR RAIN

Two days had passed since they had completely run out of water. They had used up all fruits and vegetables weeks ago, and now all that remained was oil, grains and salted meat—none of which could be eaten without some means of water. Every bit of liquid, apart from the oil, had been consumed. Severely dehydrated and suffering from heat stroke, the dry bread and salted meat was of little use. Not only were the soldiers standing on the brink of death, but so were the horses. There was talk of slaughtering and eating them. Fresh meat would have been far easier to consume without water, than dried or salted, but Seth refused.

Ophellius and his men were struggling to maintain their posts. Some of his guards were starting to collapse and die, as were some of the guards and soldiers outside.

"Now, they die of thirst," *Destroyer* triumphantly stated, as he and Lucifer stood on the fortress wall, looking down at the camp.

"Indeed," Lucifer replied. He turned his gaze towards the storehouse where Seth and 200 of his men along with their families had gathered. Crouching down, the Prince of Darkness murmured, observantly, "What are they up to?"

Seth looked around the room. "We are out of water. We cannot survive another day in the desert without it," he said grimly. "We have to come to a decision." He glanced at Zoltan, whom he had also called to this meeting. Over the weeks, he seemed to have formed a brotherly bond with him.

Weary and parched, a man named Tamon noted, "We have food."

"What good is food without water?" asked one of the women, named Ishkol. "In this heat...people are dying of thirst."

Tamon's brother, Timmon insisted, "I say we kill some of the horses and drink their blood, they're going to die anyways!"

"Drinking blood is forbidden by the law of God!" Seth disputed, "Besides, we are going to need them."

"What are you proposing? That we fight the Parthian?" Timmon asked, "We barely have the strength to stand, let alone fight."

"No. I propose that we leave," Seth replied, looking around at them. They all stared at him as though he was mad.

"You want to leave? With the Parthian army camped out in the valley?" Tamon asked.

"Where would we go?" asked Ishkol.

"Head for Arabia," Seth answered, trying to reassure them.

"Arabia!" Timmon scoffed weakly. "You really have lost your mind. We won't last a day out in that desert."

"We only need get to Petra. My cousin, King Malchus, will take us in."

"Seth," Pheroras called over their murmuring voices, "We cannot leave our mother and sister."

Seth looked at his younger brother, "I have no intention of leaving them."

"And what about the others?" he asked. "If we leave Herod's family, he will never forgive us."

"We will take the royal family with us," he assured him.

Some of the others disagreed. "Antigonus is after the royal family!" Tamon disputed, "If we take them with us, we might as well paint a target on our backs."

Pheroras insisted, "We're not leaving them!"

"Even if we were to get away..." Ishkol grumbled, "How far do you think we'd get on those horses? They are as much in need of water as we are."

Frustrated, Seth looked at Zoltan and asked, "What do you say, Zoltan?"

As the room quieted, Zoltan shrugged, "I cannot tell you whether you should go or stay, but lord Herod charged me with protecting his family and fighting our enemy. Be it here or out there, I will fight with my dying breath to protect them."

Again, the others started arguing, some for and some against it. "Look!" Seth shouted, "I am not going to stay here and watch everyone die. We are not strong enough to fight the enemy, and we've been three days without water, so come sunrise, I am taking the royal family and leaving! The rest of you can come or stay, but I'd rather take my chance out there, than face a slow death in here!"

"Then you're condemning us to death," Tamon murmured. "We might as well surrender."

Seth glared at him and warned, "Surrender and we all die. The Parthians will kill every male and enslave your wives and daughters. At least my way, we stand a chance."

Lucifer stood up and ordered, "The moment those gates open, have the Parthians slaughter them all."

"And what of Herod, when he discovers his family dead?" *Destroyer* asked.

Lucifer smiled to himself and answered, "He will seek vengeance and blood."

****

When night came, unable to sleep, Princess Miriam pulled herself up. The others were either sleeping or passed out from exhaustion. Sofera started to get up, but Miriam told her to stay. It was obvious, some of them, wouldn't last another day without water, especially the servants.

Mustering her strength, she pushed open the door and walked out onto the terrace. Weak, using the pillars to steady herself, she made her way to the balcony wall and gazed out over the landscape. Beneath the glimmer of the moonlight in the clear sky, gentle waves were rolling in and receding back on the shores of the Dead Sea. Even if it were drinkable, it might as well have been a hundred miles away—they were trapped on this cursed mountain, surrounded by an enemy army who were well fed and watered. Herod may have thought Masada to be their salvation, but without water, it would be their doom.

She looked back at the women laid out on the floor, leaning against the beds and couches. She thought about Doris leaning over her son, sobbing because he was too weak to cry any longer, and the families huddled in the lower tiers. With little hope of Herod returning in time to save them, the princess lifted her gaze towards the sky. She lifted her hands in worship, closed her eyes and quietly prayed, "Lord, God of our fathers...You are worthy to be praised. Hear my cry, for we are weak, and death waits to devour us, if not by the teeth of our enemy, by thirst. There is none to save us Lord...but You. When You speak...the earth obeys. Show mercy to your servants and our children. Send rain that we may live and tell of Your mighty works." She started to cry, when she felt a cool breeze blow against her cheeks.

****

Destroyer started to say something, but Lucifer stopped him. The Prince of Darkness looked up at the night sky observing, "Something has changed."

****

A sudden crack of thunder pierced the silence. Miriam flinched. She felt a drop of water splash onto her face. She opened her eyes. Another drop of water fell, followed by another and another. Suddenly, it began to downpour. She looked up and grinning, exclaimed, "RAIN!! Thank you, Lord! Thank you!" She ran back to the door and shouted, "RAIN!! RAIN!! EVERYONE! WAKE UP! IT'S RAINING!!" One by one, the other women joined her, as did Ophellius and his men.

Hearing the men shouting, Seth pushed open the doors of his quarters and looked outside. Pleasantly met by a downpour of rain, he stepped outside. Costobarus looked at him and shouted, "RAIN! Can you believe it!" He staggered off to check on the women, finding them and their guards out on the terrace cheerfully catching and drinking the rainwater.

Everywhere, soldiers and guards were basking in the rain: some cheering, others using their hands and helmets to catch and drink the much-needed water. Pheroras rushed over to the cisterns and opening the door, watched the water streaming down inside. Overjoyed, he began to laugh.

****

Out on the upper terrace, the women held up cups, filling them with water while their guards held out their helmets to catch the rain. Servants brought out every vessel they could find, setting them beneath the streams of water running down from the capitals of the marble pillars. Alexandra lowered her cup and put it to the prince's lips. He took a sip then pushed it towards his mother; she smiled as she drank.

Doris, who had been the first outside with her child, took a cup of water from one of the servants and gulped down several mouthfuls before putting it to her child's lips for him to drink. Noticing Miriam looking at her, she hissed quietly, "What? You think God only hears your prayers?" She looked down at her son and headed back inside. Miriam said nothing; instead, she simply looked up and smiled.

Holding buckets and pitchers, Sofera and the other maids, pushed open the palace doors. As she stepped outside, she saw Zoltan standing in the rain, drenched. He looked at her and smiled. While the other servants went to place their buckets and pitchers on walls and rooftops, to collect the rain, she dropped her buckets and ran to him. Throwing her arms around his neck, and ignoring all else, she kissed him.

Amidst the celebration, Seth stepped out into the midst of the fortress. Cupping his hands, he brought a handful of water to his parched lips and drank. Falling to his knees, he lifted his hands and looked up. Both laughing and crying, he cried aloud, "GOD BE PRAISED! WE ARE SAVED!!"

****

Awakened by a patter on his tent in the valley below, King Antigonus got up and stepped outside to discover that it was pouring down with rain. He looked across at Prince Pacorus who was listening to the cheers echoing from the fortress. He growled with disbelief, "Your God has sent them...rain." He lowered his gaze. Glaring at Antigonus as though it was somehow his fault, he railed furiously, "He sent them RAIN!!" Enraged, he shoved a guard out of the way and stormed back to his tent.

****

Lucifer looked at *Destroyer* and scowled, "Tomorrow, I want them dead!" He dove off the wall, and plummeting toward the ground, disappeared back into the Dark Realm.

****

Come morning, when the rain had subsided, the Parthians were awakened by a roaring shout: Seth and his men were leading the charge against the camp, cutting down the enemy with savage strength.

Prince Pacorus scrambled from his tent and joined Antigonus and Zahid who were staring at the battle in disbelief. "Where did these warriors come from?" Pacorus asked, as his armor bearer hurried behind him, latching his breastplate.

Antigonus pointed to the mountain. "The fortress."

"That is impossible! Weren't those men on the verge of death?"

The king put on his helmet and snarled, "Do they look like dying men to you?" He mounted his horse, drew his sword and raced into battle.

When the rain had finally come, Seth had taken it as a sign from God, and not just because it saved them. He watched each of his men stand up after drinking the rainwater. It hadn't just quenched their thirst, it had strengthened them as he'd never seen before. Infused with a supernatural strength, they were now ready and eager to fight. Taking it as a Divine sign, Seth launched the attack. Just before dawn, he and 600 warriors had made their way down the pathways into the enemy camp and began slaughtering them in their sleep. Never expecting them to recover so quickly, the Parthians awakened to find themselves under attack.

Antigonus could hardly believe these were the men who were practically dying of thirst the day before; he had witnessed several fall off the walls. Yet, here they were—a force to be reckoned with—as each man fought with the strength of ten.

24

ROMANS

Upon finally arriving in Rome, Herod paid Mark Antony a visit. After apprising him of their dire situation, he was promptly ushered into the presence of the Roman Senate to plead his case. "Jerusalem is in a state of disarray!" he exclaimed, looking up at Caesar and the other senators from the marble floor.

"I fail to see why you have brought this matter before us. This civil war between the sons of Queen Salome Alexandra has been going on for decades," Caesar huffed with a rather disinterested glance in Herod's direction, as he picked around the fruit platter being held before him. "Rome's Empire stretches across half the world; surely you cannot expect the Senate to resolve the civil affairs of every province. That is why we allow our subjects to rule themselves. Providing they keep our laws and pay their taxes, there is little we concern ourselves with outside of our domestic affairs."

"The rebel Antigonus has banded together with the Parthians to take the kingdom by force," Herod insisted.

"Parthians!" Caesar scoffed, "They hardly pose a threat to the Empire." He stuffed a handful of grapes into his mouth.

"Perhaps not on their own, but..."

"If you cannot drive out a few barbarians from your land, then perhaps I should send a Roman prefect to govern Judea," Caesar snapped.

"Your Eminence, I assure you, we Jews are quite capable of ruling ourselves," Herod answered with a hint of cold sarcasm. "All I need is a Roman army to retake the capital."

"All he needs is a Roman army!!" The Emperor blurted, looking around at the other senators and laughing. "That is no small request, nor is it cheap."

Herod looked at Althazar. The advisor clapped his hands. Immediately, two of his men rushed in carrying the large chest of gold. They placed it down at the foot of the steps before Caesar and opened it. "I take it, this should suffice," Herod remarked boldly.

Caesar shifted his eyes from the chest to Herod and with a greedy smirk answered, "Governor, you shall have your army." A Roman guard approached and whispered in Caesar's ear. "Well, it seems an army is already on its way to rescue your kin, courtesy of Mark Antony," Caesar announced glancing at Antony.

"I received a letter from him some weeks ago," Mark Antony explained.

Herod glanced at Althazar and his uncle Joseph then asked, "How many men, Your Eminence?"

Caesar looked at Mark Antony who replied, "10,000, under General Ventidius."

"You have my gratitude, Great Caesar, Senate," Herod said graciously, looking around. "But before I depart, there is another matter I must discuss."

"Oh? And what is that?"

"With King Hyrcanus taken prisoner, once Antigonus has been overthrown, Jerusalem will need a new king. "

****

Although Seth had left Ophellius and Costobarus in charge of 100 men inside the fortress to guard the royal family, the commanders and the 600 men he brought down to the camp, were more than holding their own against thousands of Parthian troops. They had slaughtered over a thousand of Antigonus' men—

with skills that were unmatched. Zoltan alone took out over 100. They were starting to drive them back, unaware that king Antigonus was luring them into a trap. The enemy had divided their troops, and at the king's signal, Prince Pacorus brought his men up at the rear, closing them in. By the time Seth realized, his men were completely surrounded.

Perched on a crag above, *Destroyer*— overseeing the enemy's strategy—fixed his black eyes on one target—Seth. The moment the snare closed in around him, the large demon, clad in iron with his black wings blowing in the wind, stood up and lifted his clawed hands, summoning a black whirling mist—death. Like a swirling ball of black flames kindling over a red-hot coal, he lined it up with Seth's heart; while directly beneath him, like the puppet—and *Destroyer* the puppet-master— Prince Pacorus lined up an arrow.

Realizing they had fallen into an ambush, Seth and his men braced themselves to fight their way out, or fight to the death. With the commander in his sights, Prince Pacorus pulled back on his bow.

"LOOK!!" Zahid shouted, pointing towards the hills. All eyes turned towards the highlands as he heralded, "ROMANS!!" The unmistakable sea of crimson robes and glimmering armor was emerging from a nearby ridge.

As the alarm went out, the Parthians ceased fighting. *Destroyer* looked back, saw the army, and with a snarled scowl, disappeared in a whiff of black smoke. With him, went the enemy's courage. Upon seeing the Romans riding into battle, Pacorus lowered his bow and fled. His men followed. And though reluctantly, when King Antigonus and his men saw the others fleeing, they too fled the area.

Seth's men cheered as the Romans chased after their enemy, parting around them like water flowing around a rock. As the sea of red cloaks parted around the small army to Seth's men, their commander stopped with a handful of men and asked, "Who is in charge?"

"I am," Seth answered, riding forward. "I am Commander Seth, brother to Governor Herod."

The Roman commander—dressed in a red robe, scaled breastplate and helmet—said with an arrogant smile, "I am General Ventidius, and this is my second, Commander Silo. We have orders to assist you."

25

THE TIDES OF CHANGE

Sometime after the Romans' arrival, Doris awakened upon hearing a vile whisper in her ear. Whether she had dreamed it or heard it, she couldn't tell, but *Malice* had awoken her.

General Ventidius and Commander Silo had taken most of the Roman army and camped outside of Jerusalem, but he had left a small contingent of a thousand men to guard Masada.

Miriam stood on the terrace between two of the marble pillars that encircled the palace. She glanced at the pair of Roman guards, positioned by the steps leading to the lower terrace. She smiled, but her smile soon faded. Her thoughts ran to Herod, wondering if he had made it safely to Rome. With the fortress under siege, they hadn't heard anything else from him since the day Zoltan and Sofera had arrived. Wrapped up in her thoughts, Miriam didn't hear the soft footsteps creeping up and coming to a stop a few feet behind her. She didn't feel the icy stare piercing the back of her head, nor did she sense a pair of hands slowly beginning to rise and reach towards her back.

"He's here! He's here!" Pheroras shouted from the tower, spotting an army crossing the valley, and a familiar face at the head of them. "Herod has returned!!"

Miriam turned around, hearing the patter of feet and seeing a flash of color running back inside. Wondering who had been outside with her, she looked around then hurried inside. Doris walked past with her maids, deciding on a dress. "Were you just outside?" Miriam enquired.

Doris looked at her strangely and muttered dismissively, "I don't know what you are talking about." She quickly turned her attention to her maid as they held up a variety of dresses for her to choose from. Miriam eyed her suspiciously then walked off while a devious smirk crept over Doris' face.

"Lord Herod has brought an army!!" Prince Aris shouted back as he peered over the wall. He quickly climbed down and joined his mother in the dusty courtyard where guards were opening the gates. Riding on a black stallion to the deafening roar of cheers, Herod's return was nothing short of triumphant. He had come back with an army comprised of Romans, and Jews gathered along the way, whose numbers stretched all the way down into the valley. It was long overdue and a welcomed sight for everyone—or almost everyone. Alexandra watched him enter, anxious to hear Caesar's decree regarding her son.

Upon climbing down off his horse, Herod first greeted his brothers in a tearful embrace. He also reached over and squeezed Costobarus' shoulder. However, they were all pushed aside by Doris, barging in with his son. Not caring what anyone said, she greeted her husband with a passionate kiss. The men whistled and cheered. Relieved to see them safe, he held her in a long embrace, whispering. "I feared I had lost you both."

"You would have, if not for the Romans," she replied, then handed Herod his young son.

"Dadda!" the boy exclaimed. He then proceeded to tell his father all that had happened in a garble of indistinguishable words that only a two-year old would understand.

"Antipater!" He kissed him on the forehead, uttering, "My son! You've grown!" Herod rested his face against his son's. He took comfort in the familiar smell of his skin, the feel of his small hands squeezing his face and the sound of his voice, giggling and laughing. He then greeted Cypros and Salome.

Salome then turned her gaze towards Costobarus, while Cypros whispered in Herod's ear, "Is it done?"

He was about to answer when his eye caught a glimpse of something vibrant blue, blowing in the breeze. His smile fading, Herod handed the child back to Doris. He stepped past his mother and looked through the parting crowd. Standing there in a sea-blue silk dress, trimmed with gold, was Princess Miriam. Haloed by the bright sun, her hair and vale were blowing gently in the breeze. She greeted him with a gentle smile. Mesmerized, Herod was drawn to her, oblivious of the jealous scowl on Doris' face. Miriam glanced at her, and at that moment, Doris knew the dress was payback for the evil she had intended out on the terrace.

Squeezing Zoltan's shoulder as he passed him, Herod took Miriam's hand and pressed his lips against it. "I knew you would return to me," she said, gently caressing his face.

He kissed her and held her, smelling the soft scent of jasmine in her hair and the fragrant oils on her skin. "I had forgotten how beautiful you are."

Someone clearing their throat interrupted the moment. Herod shifted his gaze past Miriam to Alexandra and the young prince standing beside her, eagerly watching him. "My lord, Herod," she called pretentiously.

"Princess Alexandra and young Prince Aris. I am pleased to see you both in good health." Herod started walking towards the large palace entrance.

"I knew you would return! I never doubted it!" Aris said excitedly.

"You and I both," Herod said, rubbing his head as he walked past.

"Am I king now?" the boy asked aloud. Herod halted. Everyone grew quiet. "Am I?" The boy asked again. "Did Caesar make me king?"

Herod looked around at the men, and then turned to face the boy and his mother. After a moment of hesitation and a heavy sigh, he replied, "It has been a long journey. My men are tired, hungry and thirsty. Let us eat and rest. We will discuss politics later." He turned his attention back to his men as they headed towards the palace.

"My lord!" Alexandra called. "The boy has waited many days and endured much hardship and danger while awaiting your return; surely, you can spare a moment to answer his question."

Her words brought Herod to a grinding halt. An awkward silence fell over the camp. Herod glanced at Sohemus and his uncle Joseph. With a slightly annoyed sigh, he turned around and begrudgingly answered. "Well, if the boy waited this long, then a few more hours should be of no consequence."

As he turned to walk away, Alexandra demanded, "Why? How hard of a question is it to answer? Did Caesar proclaim my son, king! Yes or no?"

Herod halted and looked around at the men, realizing that all were awaiting his answer; he turned around and replied, "No."

"NO!" she shrieked.

"No. He did not proclaim your son, king."

"Why not?"

His eyes narrowing, trying to temper his response, Herod answered, "There are many reasons, none of which I am prepared to discuss at this moment."

Pushing her son behind her, Alexandra stepped forward and belligerently demanded, "Then who is to be king of Judea?"

Glancing around at the others, pondering his response, Herod breathed a heavy sigh and replied, "I am."

Alexandra's mouth fell open. Not a sound was heard, except the howling of the wind blowing atop the mountain, until the silence was suddenly broken by Seth shouting, "ALL HAIL KING HEROD! ALL HAIL KING HEROD!"

Sohemus and Hippicus lifted their swords and joined Seth, stirring the rest of the camp to a rousing cheer. Herod and Princess Alexandra stared down one another, until the men lifted him on their shoulders and carried him off, leaving her and her son standing in the dust—despondent.

"If he is king..." Prince Aris asked, "Then what am I?"

26

THE OCTOPUS AND THE SNAKE

Herod sat at the head of the royal table, holding his golden goblet and staring aimlessly at Alexandra, seated at the opposite end of the table, glaring at him. The room was full of chatter, laughter and music. Roman commanders were exchanging tales of heroic battles with Herod's commanders. The young prince—seated adjacent to his mother—timidly picked at his food, glancing up at her every now and again. "So, King Herod..." Alexandra hissed loudly. "Tell us, how is it, you manage to claim the throne, you promised my son?"

The room fell deafly silent. All eyes turned to Herod, awaiting his answer. Herod's mind ran back to the events that had taken place at Rome's Senate.

****

"So, who do you recommend to be King of the Jews?" Caesar asked, taking a sloppy sip of wine. "Does Hyrcanus not have an heir?"

"Yes," Herod replied, "A grandson, but he is just a boy."

Glassy-eyed, Caesar shrugged and enquired, "In your opinion, is he ready to rule?"

Herod shifted a glance to his uncle and Althazar. Both men nodded. Contemplating his mother's words, staring at an area of empty seats in the descending benches of the circular Senate, Herod hesitated.

"Well Governor?" Caesar demanded, casting a cold glance at his servant as he hurried to pour him more wine. "Are you here to request that I name the boy, King of the Jews?"

Herod shifted his gaze back to the Emperor and replied, "No. I have come to claim the throne."

The hall fell silent. "You?" Caesar looked around the Senate in surprise.

"Yes, me."

There was a moment of awkward silence. "Are you not the one they begrudging call Half-Jew?" the Emperor sniped. "If I appoint you king instead of their prince, surely these people will rise up in rebellion."

"Your Eminence, the people are already in rebellion," Herod answered formidably. "What the kingdom needs, is stability."

"And you believe you can bring that stability?"

"I do."

"So do I," Mark Antony announced, standing up. *"Perhaps the country would best benefit with a man of experience on the throne. Herod is already governor of Galilee."* He turned his gaze to Herod and strolled down the steps. *"How many of our allies are as skilled in battle, wise in rule and loyal to Rome as he? Few, I dare say."* Resting his hand on Herod's shoulder, he looked back up at the Emperor and declared, *"So, when such a man stands before the Senate, ready to rule, would not prudence demand that we place him in power?"*

"You make a compelling argument, General," Caesar acknowledged, while many of the other senators nodded in agreement. *"But, tell me Governor...what do you intend to do with the boy?"*

Herod shrugged. *"I am betrothed to his sister. He and his mother are my kin. Therefore, they will remain under my protection."*

Pondering, Caesar looked around at the Senate and asked, *"Is the Senate in agreement? Should this man be named King of the Jews?"*

One by one, each member of the Senate raised their hands, until every hand was raised. Caesar turned his gaze back to Herod. Rising to his feet, he announced, *"Then I, Caesar, Emperor of the Rome, declare from this day forth, you shall be known as Herod the Great! King of the Jews!"*

The moment it was pronounced, the empty seating appeared to move. Camouflaged among the benches, Greed slithered up and along the walls. She had been tracking Herod. From the moment his mother had whispered in his ear on the day he'd left Masada, Greed had been trailing him—poisoning his heart with whispers of her own. And now that Caesar had declared him King of the Jews, her work was done. She slipped back into the shadows while servants placed a purple robe, trimmed with gold, on Herod shoulders—a symbolic acknowledgement of his kingship—along with a jewel encrusted sword, given to him by Caesar himself.

Hearing their adulation ringing in his ears, Herod looked up at the Senate and smiled. He brought his eyes to rest on Mark Antony. Looking down on him, Antony was thinking about the sack of gold Herod had paid him for his support before entering the Senate.

"Now you have an army and a kingdom..." Caesar announced over their cheers. "Go claim your throne!"

****

Herod turned his gaze back to Alexandra and opened his mouth to speak, but breaking the silence, Cypros replied, "You need not answer that."

"Why not?" Princess Alexandra insisted sharply.

Cypros put down her food and glaring at her, replied, "Because he is not on trial! Like it or not, he is your king! Show respect!" Returning to her meal, she murmured, "What is done is done."

Alexandra stared at her for a moment, then scowled, "Oh yes, how fortunate for you. After all these years of serving my father...I suppose you finally got what you wanted—your son is king instead of mine!" Again, the room fell into an awkward silence. Hippicus and Sohemus glanced at one another, and then looked from Alexandra to Herod—as did everyone else.

Calmly putting her cup to her lips, Cypros said quietly, "Please Alexandra, do not embarrass yourself or the boy."

"Embarrass the boy!" she railed, standing up. "My son—THE RIGHTFUL HEIR—was promised the kingdom! Only to have it snatched from him by the very man, who gave his word that *he* was going to Rome to have Caesar declare him king! How much more humiliation can we bare!!"

"ALEXANDRA!" Herod bellowed, "Your son is a child! A mere boy! Can I help it if Caesar felt the kingdom needed a more stable hand?"

"And you were just ready to step into his sandals! Or rather his throne!" She raised her cup and with a loathsome scowl, sneered, "Well, ALL HAIL OUR KING! Never has Judea seen a more cunning and treacherous king upon her throne!"

"Mother!" Princess Miriam shrieked, trying to calm her down, but Alexandra ignored her.

"From slave to master!! And master to slave! LONG LIVE KING HEROD!!" she snarled then poured out her drink on the floor and threw the cup to the ground.

"ENOUGH!!" Herod shouted, standing up and banging his fists on the table. "Everyone...OUT!!"

The room quickly cleared with a rush of shuffling feet and hushed whispers, until only Herod and Alexandra remained. When the door closed behind Miriam and the young prince, Herod snarled, "How dare you!!"

"How dare I? How dare you! A mere servant, presume to steal my son's throne!!"

"I am NO-ONE'S servant!"

"You were servant to my father! As was your father!"

Thwarted by her statement, Herod glared at her and replied smugly, "And now, I am your king! And I did not steal the throne, it was given to me!"

Alexandra stormed towards him railing, "Given! Because you are a man without honor! The son of slaves and cutthroats! Unworthy of our throne!!"

"Mind your tongue!" he hissed narrowing his eyes. "If not for Miriam, I would have you imprisoned for speaking such treasonous words!!"

The two of them glared at one another like angry bulls. Finally, deciding to take a calmer approach, Herod straightened his garments and strutted across to the window. "It was never my intention to seek the throne. I went to Rome to make the boy, king."

"Yet, here you are...King of the Jews," she snarled sarcastically.

"The boy's ascension would only have weakened Judea! Can you not see that? Our enemies would have looked on him the way a lion looks on its prey. He has neither the strength nor wisdom to rule. What I did, was for the good of the kingdom!"

"The good of the kingdom?" The princess laughed. "No, my lord, what you did, you did for yourself. I saw it in your eyes, the day you left. I knew then, what I know now...you are a snake! Full of greed and envy! You did not go to Rome to claim the throne for my son; you went to claim it for yourself! And had I sent my son with you, he would have NEVER returned. You would have told me, he perished at sea! But we would both know the truth!"

Herod stared at her, offended. "My lady, I do not murder the innocent. I love the boy as though he were my own son. I would never harm him."

"Then what is to become of him?"

Herod shook his head. "Nothing. Miriam will be Queen of Judea, and you and your son will remain in the palace as my kin. When he is of age...I will find him a suitable region to govern."

"Govern? Well, how gracious of you, my lord," she scowled, before heading towards the door.

Herod turned and forcefully asserted, "Whether you like it or not, Alexandra! I am your king! From this day on, you will treat me with the proper respect, or I shall have you thrown in the dungeons until you do. Have I made myself clear?"

Princess Alexandra turned, and bowing her head, hissed with a facetious smile, "Yes, my lord." Her smile fading into an icy scowl, she headed through the door and slammed it behind her.

27

SABOTAGE

Hearing that Ventidius was in Jerusalem with the rest of his Roman troops, after a day's rest, Herod left Masada. He took with him the royal family and his newfound army, leaving a small contingent of men to guard the fortress. Jerusalem, however, was not his destination, at least not yet. First, he needed to increase their numbers and drive out the enemy from the surrounding towns and villages before heading to the capital.

Standing on the highest point of the palace in Masada with the five ancient demons at his side, watching Herod leave, Lucifer remarked, "I believe it is time to sever another cord." He motioned to *Destroyer*. "See to it."

"With pleasure," the demon growled. He, in turn, glanced to his left and called, "*Greed*, you're up." Spreading his black wings, *Destroyer* took to the air. *Greed*—growing to a gargantuan size—stretched her long tentacles until they touched the floor of the valley below, then stepped down off the pinnacle. Moving like an octopus across the seabed, invisible to men's eyes, she traversed great distances, changing colors with the passing clouds and landscape.

A minute later, *Destroyer* landed on the top of the mountain overlooking the Roman camp on the plains outside of Jerusalem. *Greed* soon slithered up beside him. Surveying the camp and spotting the general's tent, at *Destroyer's* order, *Greed* stretched out her tentacles and pulled herself over to the general's tent, enveloping it as she slithered inside.

****

A servant came into the throne room and handed Itiel a letter. He handed it to the king. Upon opening it, Antigonus' face contorted. "That Roman pig, Ventidius wants 500 talents of gold, or he's threatening to attack the city!" Frustrated he got up, crumpling the letter in his hand. "Where do they expect me to find all this money? I'm already paying them to keep out of the city, and now they want more!"

While he walked by the windows grumbling, two more messengers arrived. One went to Prince Pacorus, the other to Zahid. Upon hearing his report, Zahid looked at the messenger startled. He looked at the irate king and hesitantly approached him. "My lord, I have received a report...it's about Herod."

"What is it now?" Antigonus grunted. Zahid stared at him nervously. "Well, man, speak!"

Lowering his eyes, Zahid nervously reported, "Caesar has declared him...King of the Jews."

"WHAT!!" His eyes bulging, Antigonus looked liked he was about to pop a vein. "How could he name that Half-Jew our king? I am the KING!"

"I'm afraid, that is not the only bad news you will hear today, my friend," Prince Pacorus announced, getting up. He sent his servants to gather his things. "War has come to Parthia," he said soberly. "I must defend our kingdom." He called to one of his guards, "Gather the troops, we're leaving." He then gestured for his armor-bearer to bring his armor.

His world suddenly crumbling around him, King Antigonus called, "Wait! You're leaving?"

"Yes. You have your kingdom, now I must defend mine."

Antigonus brushed his hands threw his hair in frustration. He hurried down the steps towards the prince. "But...you...you cannot leave now! What about the Romans? They are threatening to invade!"

"They have invaded my land! If I do not defend against them, my people and I will have no home! We will be their subjects!" Pacorus shouted sternly. "We will not become their slaves!" He stared at Antigonus. "At least you have a choice. Pay them or fight them, but whatever you choose, you will have to do it alone. War calls, and I must answer."

"But...but how am I to fight Herod without you?"

Prince Pacorus grabbed the king's arms and staring into his face, said intensely, "When I have driven the Romans from my land, I will come back and help you drive Herod from yours. But if I do not...you are a resourceful man...you will find a way." He held out his arm to the king.

With a heavy sigh, Antigonus clasped his forearm and embraced him. "God be with you."

"We will meet again, my friend," the prince assured him as he headed for the door, "If not in this life...then in the next!"

King Antigonus watched the Parthian prince and all his men leave. Gathering all his horses and troops, they exited on one side of the city while the Romans encamped on the other. In a fit of rage, Antigonus shrieked while kicking over several chairs and tables. When he had broken everything in sight—apart from the throne—he looked at Itiel and Zahid, both of whom had moved out of the range of flying objects. "Send for Babas!" he shouted. "And inform the Council, I will be doubling the taxes!"

****

After driving the enemy out of the surrounding countryside, Herod arrived at Jerusalem some weeks later with a vast army. Although many were farmers and tradesmen, with the addition of 9,000 Roman troops, there was no doubt that victory was now within his grasp. But upon arrival, he found that things were not as expected.

"What do you mean, 'gone'?" Herod growled.

Commander Silo shrugged. "The general said he was needed at war and left. Who am I to question him?"

"He was hired to fight this war! MY WAR!!" Herod raged, frustrated. "How many men did he take?"

Silo shrugged and reluctantly answered, "6,000."

"6,000!!" With his men standing outside his tent, Herod's commanders cringed as they listened to him blast the Roman commander. He was livid. "10, 000 ROMANS!! That is what I paid for!! 10,000! NOT 4...10!!" he railed, dramatically holding up his fingers as though the commander was incapable of counting. "How am I supposed to retake Jerusalem with only 4,000 Romans?" Enraged, he picked up a jug of wine and hurled it at the tent post, narrowly missing Hippicus' head, as he ducked out of the way.

"Do you forget, lord Herod, we are Romans?" Silo pointed out in a patronizing tone. "The general left me here with 3,000 of his most skilled fighters! If we join with the thousand you have, and your own men, we can take this city!"

Herod glared at the commander. He was not convinced. After a long pause, he scowled, "What choice has he left me? But I assure you, Caesar will hear of this injustice!"

Silo muttered under his breath, "I am sure he will." As Herod turned to face him, the Roman commander asked, "So…what's the plan?"

Herod looked around at his commanders. "Half of those men out there are little more than farmers and tradesmen. Since I am missing more than half of my Roman army, the first thing we do, is train them to fight.

With Romans being among the most skilled and proficient fighters in the known world, Herod assigned them—along with his most skillful Jewish soldiers—to train the new recruits. Many of the Romans complied, but the rest sat around complaining as their supplies dwindled. Each day those complaints grew louder.

Upon promising to meet their demands, Herod sent for a convoy of food and supplies. It never reached. The enemy attacked. They stole everything and killed everyone, leaving only one man alive to spread the news to the other merchants. The same thing happened the next time, and the next. Even when they switched to secret routes, it seemed the enemy somehow knew when and where to find them.

Early one morning, as they prepared for battle, Herod was awakened by the blast of a ram's horn. He rushed outside. The Romans were packing up. "What is going on?"

"They're leaving!" Hippicus growled frustrated.

"What do you mean, 'leaving'?" Herod asked. Hippicus gestured to the commander supervising his servants as they packed up his tent. "Ask him."

Herod marched over to him and demanded, "Commander Silo! What is the meaning of this?"

Silo looked at him and nonchalantly answered, "You promised us supplies. There are no supplies, so now, my men and I are leaving."

"You will have your supplies!"

"Oh yeah? From where? Antigonus has ambushed every convoy that has tried to get through. Now everyone is too afraid." He showed Herod a pair of the soldiers' sandals with holes in the bottom. "Winter is coming. Their shoes are worn, their cloaks and tunics falling apart! I will not send my men to fight your war starving and naked!"

Desperate, Herod responded, "We will share what we have!"

Silo checked the line, securing his bed and tent on his packhorse, whilst muttering, "You barely have enough to feed your own men, let alone mine. Besides, Romans do not wear the clothing of their subjects into battle." With everything secured, the commander climbed up onto his horse. "Tell you what, my men and I will go and find us somewhere warm and dry to hold up for the winter. We'll be back in the spring. Perhaps, by then, you will have figured out how to get your supplies through...if you haven't starved by then," he muttered.

Irate, Herod raged, "YOU ARE UNDER MY COMMAND!! AND WE ARE TAKING THAT CITY!!"

Silo looked down at Herod and said with a smug smirk, "You go right ahead. But my men are under my command, and I say, we're leaving." With a tug on his horse's reins and a facetious salute, the commander rode off.

Devastated, Herod looked at Jerusalem, and then turned his eyes towards Commander Silo. Livid, he drew his sword and went after him, but his uncle, Sohemus and Hippicus held him back. "No! Herod!" Joseph begged. "Do this and everything will have been for nothing!"

"They will kill you, and make slaves of your family!" Sohemus growled, dragging him back.

Glaring into his face, Hippicus shouted, "Antigonus will win! Is that what you want?"

With reason slowly sinking in, Herod's uncontrollable fury began to fizzle. The last thing he wanted was to give Antigonus the victory, especially after killing his brother. He slowly lowered his sword, but as he watched his hopes riding off, in a sudden fit of rage, Herod swung his sword and with a bellowing roar, lopped the head off a nearby horse. The animal let out an agonizing wail then went down, spewing blood everywhere. Herod continued to hack at its neck. Silo glanced back and snickering, rode off to join the rest of his army.

"What was that?" asked Miriam, hearing the commotion from inside their tent. She went to peer out, but Cypros—who had witnessed the altercation—not wanting her to see what her future husband had done in his rage, met her at the entrance.

"It's nothing. One of the animals took a fall, that's all." She ushered Miriam back inside, while Salome—who had seen the whole thing—stared at her brother with a cold chill running down her spine. She had never seen him so enraged.

Long after the Romans had left, covered in the animal's blood, Herod stood over a bronze basin, washing it off. His commanders watched him in silence before glancing at one another, deciding who should speak first; his uncle finally said, "Nephew, we cannot attack the city without the Romans. If you try, your troops will abandon you."

Seth walked in, dragging in a palace servant. He threw him down and ordered, "Tell him what you know."

Trembling, the servant answered, "My lord, I saw Prince Antigonus give the Roman general gold, just before he left with his army. Then I saw the prince send more gold with one of his servants."

"Tell him where he sent it," Seth ordered.

"I overheard him say it was to be given to Commander Silo in payment for feeding him information."

Glaring at him, Herod growled, "What information?"

Shaking and stuttering as his teeth chattered, the servant answered, "The supply routes, and your plan of attack."

Sohemus pushed the servant aside and scowled, "ROMAN SCUM!! They betrayed you!!"

"Both of them!" Herod scowled, wringing his towel. He threw it down and snarled, "They never had any intention of fighting our enemy!"

Questioning the validity of the report, Joseph looked at the servant and asked Seth, "Where did you find this man?"

"Zoltan. He has friends inside the city, tradesmen," Seth replied. "He got word to them, and had them spy on the palace. When they found this one in the market, they smuggled him out and brought him to us."

"Where did Antigonus get gold to give to the Romans?" Herod demanded.

The servant replied, "Babas and his sons. He has convinced many of the noble houses to support the k..." Seeing the rage in Herod's eyes, the servant said, "the usurper."

Overturning his table, spilling wine, food and water everywhere, Herod raged, "Is there no end to the treachery against me!"

"Herod..." Hippicus called, "if we cannot attack Jerusalem, what are we to do?"

With cold and ruthless eyes, Herod looked out through the tent entrance, across the plains to the distant hills in the East. "We're going to Arabia, I'm going to get my gold back from Malchus."

"No, Brother, you are not," Seth said, bravely stepping forward. "You are king. If you leave Judea now, all those you have gained will go back to their homes. You must stay here and continue to gather men. I will go. Give me 2,000 men, and I will give you Arabia. And if Malchus refuses...I will bring you his head."

Herod stared at his brother. Impressed by his tenacity, he smiled and resting his hand on Seth's shoulder, nodded in agreement.

28

HILL OF THE DEAD

It had been some time since Commander Seth had left to subdue Arabia. Herod had also sent his uncle Joseph with a large number of his troops to build siege ramps, while he took the rest of his army to assist General Mark Antony in battle. Upon returning, he was awakened one winter's morning hearing his name being called. "King Herod!! Herod!!" Sohemus pushed open the entrance of his tent. His face pale and grim, he murmured, "We need you."

Herod followed him outside, passing through a line of men. As the commander led him to a cart and stepped aside, his heart began to pound. Herod looked down at the bloodied white linen cloth. He then looked across at Hippicus and his brother, Pheroras; tears were streaming down their faces. Herod looked down at the body. His hands trembling, he slowly lifted the cloth. The body that lay beneath was headless. "My patrol found him in a valley near Jericho," Zoltan reported in a deeply remorseful tone. "He and his men had been slaughtered. I recognized the scare on his arm."

Herod lifted the cloth further and saw the diagonal scare on Seth's left arm, along with his armor; it was the same armor Seth had been wearing when he left. Shuddering, and tearing his garments, Herod shrieked, "NOOO!!!" His agonizing cries echoed through the camp.

His mother, sister and the other women came running. Costobarus and Joseph stopped them in their tracks.

"Don't look!" Joseph insisted, but Cypros pushed him aside and ran to the body.

When she saw Seth's headless corpse, she fell onto his chest and wept, "NO! MY SON! MY SON!!"

Salome screamed hysterically, "Where is his head?"

"This is how they found him," Costobarus explained, holding her, trying to calm her.

Bawling, she sobbed in his arms, "They took his head!"

Sofera had remained in the tent with the children while Doris fell to her knees, sobbing dramatically, and Alexandra—staring coldly at them—held onto Miriam as she buried her face and wept.

Herod tried to comfort his mother, but as his grief turned to anger and his eyes filled with rage; he looked at Zoltan and snarled, "Who took my BROTHER'S HEAD!!"

"Farmers reported seeing Antigonus at the site, my lord." With a heavy sigh, and blinking away the tears stinging his eyes, he reported, "They saw him...cut off his head, but he was already dead. I only wish my men had gotten there earlier."

"Who killed him?" Herod raged. "Was it Malchus?"

"No," Hippicus reported, "Malchus yielded. Seth returned with the gold and the crown. Antigonus sent troops against them. They were led by a man named Pappus; it was he who killed Seth."

Sohemus added, "There are also reports that the Galileans have revolted and drowned the commanders you put over them."

Herod rested his hand on Zoltan's shoulder. Overwhelmed with grief, he looked at him through a blur of tears. Zoltan rested his hand on his and said with a heavy sigh, "Seth was my friend. He was a good man."

Herod nodded. He turned to the rest of them and ordered, "Tell the men to pack up. We're moving out!"

"What about Jerusalem, my lord?" Costobarus asked.

Herod scowled. "Jerusalem can wait. I want vengeance! I want Pappus!"

****

Destroyer joined Lucifer as he stood under a low hanging cypress tree. He was watching a farmer ploughing his field. "Is it done?" he asked.

Destroyer replied, "Yes. I whispered in the ear of Antigonus...and he took the boy's head."

"And how did Herod react?" Lucifer asked, glancing up as several birds came and landed in its branches, chirping noisily.

"Devastated. He's on the warpath."

Lucifer smiled and muttered, "Good." He reached up into the tree. The chirping stopped. A bird dropped, followed by another and another. Suddenly they began to fall like rain, until the ground was scattered with dead birds. Lucifer muttered, "That's better." He reached into a nest and plucked out an egg, examining it as it began to decay in his hand. "Now, be sure the seeds of *Malice* continue to grow within him." As the egg turned black and withered, Lucifer crushed it between his fingers until it become dust. "I want his heart darker."

"As you wish."

Destroyer disappeared. Lucifer then turned his gaze back to the farmer. Aiming at the oxen on the plough, Lucifer twisted his hand. One of the oxen suddenly fell, taking the farmer down and injuring him as the plough twisted and broke. Lucifer chuckled to himself.

****

It took several weeks, but after hunting down those who had slaughtered his brother's army, and killing many of them, Herod finally captured Commander Pappus. With nowhere else to run, in desperation, his army fled and hid themselves in a village on a hillside. They slaughtered everyone, and hid the bodies before hiding inside the houses. Dozens upon dozens of the rebel soldiers piled inside each house, hoping to escape detection, but Herod's men discovered them. Piled on top of one another, they were huddled so tightly, they could hardly move.

Herod had Pappus brought to the hillside, and forced him to watch as his men barricaded the doors and windows of the village houses, trapping Pappus' men inside. Cypros and Salome watched from a litter. Their eyes were cold and devoid of sympathy as Herod ordered Sohemus and his men to tear off the roofs and hurl large rocks down on the enemy. With the doors and windows boarded up, there was no escape from the horrors that followed.

Hearing their screams and the sound of their fists desperately pounding and scratching on the boarded doors and windows as they tried to escape was chilling. Even worse, was the sound of their bones being broken and their skulls being crushed by the large rocks while they begged for mercy.

Pappus lowered his head and closed his eyes, grieved to his very soul, as their shrills echoed across the hillside. Those at the bottom, who managed to escape the rocks, survived only to be suffocated beneath the weight of the dead lying on top of them.

When all movement within the houses had ceased, and all their cries were silenced, Herod had Pappus brought to the foot of the hillside to watch as the bodies of his men were carried out and piled up in a giant heap. With a look from Herod, Zoltan kicked Pappus in the side of his leg, dropping him to his knees. "You were not afraid to kill my brother, and Antigonus was not afraid to take his head," Herod snarled and slowly drew his sword. "But from this day, all who see this *Hill of the Dead* will speak my name and tremble!"

In a sudden blinding rage, he lopped off the commander's head, then watched it roll down towards the hill until it came to a stop when it hit the wall of corpses. The warm blood dripping off his sword, Herod lifted his gaze to the distant hills where other enemy troops were gathering to war against them, but when they saw the gruesome hill of the dead, they fled.

29

GRATITUDE

Despite Antigonus still being in possession of Seth's head, having laid his brother to rest, and winter coming to an end, Herod returned to his palace in Samaria. He summoned all the leaders to his royal court. Seated on his throne with hundreds of commanders, nobles, priests and the royal family present, Herod looked across the room as Althazar called out Sohemus, Joseph, Hippicus, Pheroras, Costobarus and Zoltan. "Each of you, step forward," he ordered, then stepped aside.

Zoltan joined the others at the foot of the steps leading up to Herod's throne. He was not sure why he had been called among them. His heart racing, he bowed before the king. "All of you have shown extraordinary courage and loyalty. In the face of this war, each of you has proven himself to be loyal to me, and my cause," Herod declared. "Sohemus and Hippicus, my right and left hands.

Sohemus, I promote you to General. Hippicus, you are now Captain of the Royal Guards." King Herod glanced at Ophellius who had previously held that position under King Hyrcanus. "Ophellius...you will now serve as head of Prince Aris and Princess Alexandra's bodyguards!" he announced. Ophellius nodded graciously, as Herod turned his attention to Joseph. "Uncle, you have tempered my anger with reason, and with wisdom, you have given me sound counsel. There is no man's counsel, I trust more. And so, I promote you to 1st Commander." Joseph nodded.

Shifting his eyes, King Herod called, "Costobarus...the Idumean! I promote you to 2nd Commander." He looked at his younger brother, "Pheroras, you are wise beyond your years. Your mind is sharp; your heart, compassionate; and your hands are almost as skilled as mine," he said with a smile. The crowd chuckled. "When this war is over, you shall head the repairs of our cities and my fortresses." He turned his gaze. "Zoltan, you risked your life to bring me news of the death of my older brother at the hands of my enemy. You could have left my younger brother's body to rot in that valley, but instead you brought him home, so we could lay him to rest with honor. "

"I only did what any man would do for you, my lord."

"Perhaps, but you have proven yourself both loyal and valuable to my cause, and Costobarus tells me you are highly skilled with a sword." Zoltan lowered his head and smiled bashfully. "I need good men at my side, and so I promote you to 3rd Commander."

Dropping to one knee and bowing, Zoltan put his fist to his chest and said, "You honor me, my lord. I shall not let you down."

"See that you do not," Herod remarked with a cold smile. The others bowed as red robes were put onto the shoulders of the commanders, black on the general and captain of the guards and a blue sash on Pheroras. Applause quickly filled the large room as the men took their place on either side of the king. Zoltan glanced at Sofera and smiled. She was grinning from ear to ear, clapping excitedly.

Calming the crowd, Herod announced, "Now, onto other affairs. We have been at war with Antigonus for 3 years!" His expression turning to anger, he leaned forward and raged, "Can no-one tell me, how to defeat our enemy and retake Jerusalem!"

While the crowd murmured and whispered among themselves, Althazar stepped forward and announced, "I believe I can, my lord." He produced a letter bearing a Roman seal. The seal was broken. He unfurled it and read aloud, "For aiding in my conquest and assuring my victory over our enemy, you have the gratitude of Rome. I have assigned you, King Herod, not one, but several Roman legions under the command of one of my most loyal men—General Sosius. I wish you good fortune, and may your God grant you victory in your conquest. Signed, Mark Antony!" Cheers erupted throughout the court.

Herod stood up and exclaimed, "Now that! My friends, is how we shall defeat our enemy and retake our land!"

The cheers grew even louder until Herod calmed them and asked, "Uncle, are our siege ramps ready?"

"Indeed, they are, my lord," Joseph proudly announced, prompting more cheers.

"Do you know what this means?" Herod shouted excitedly, "After three years of being driven from our homes...and 30 years of civil war—when our Roman allies arrive—we shall undertake our final campaign! And then we shall recapture Jerusalem, ONCE AND FOR ALL!!"

The explosion of cheers was deafening and it rang on for what seemed like ages. Herod could not recall seeing his people in such good spirit since the war began. After several moments, he raised his hands, calming the crowd. He looked across at Miriam and extended his hand to her. Doris watched as she got up and walked past her to join him. "Now, while we wait for our Roman allies, what greater way to celebrate our impending victory, than with a marriage feast! So, may I present to you my betrothed...the beautiful Princess, and soon to be Queen Miriam!!"

Once again, the hall erupted into cheers. With the hope of victory ahead, a royal wedding was just what everyone needed. It wasn't just an event to lift their spirits, but they took it as a symbol of hope, marking the beginning of a new era. However, not everyone shared their excitement. While the crowd cheered, Alexandra sat to his left, staring coldly at Herod, and Doris, to his right, glaring at Princess Miriam. As Herod looked back at them, the two women forced a smile and clapped their hands until he looked away, then they exchanged cold glances with each other.

30

THE THORN AND THE ROSE

From the day Herod had announced his betrothal to Princess Miriam, Doris' hatred and jealously of her had been steadily growing. And now that she was queen and could lord it over them, Doris' treatment of the princess worsened. In front of Herod, she appeared civil, if not snidely condescending, but behind his back, she treated Miriam with the utmost contempt.

As the wedding drew near, the toll of the strenuous relationship was becoming more and more evident to everyone, except Herod. One evening, Salome pulled the queen aside and said quietly, "If I were you...I would be nice to her."

As she started to walk away, Doris grabbed her arm and hissed, "Who do you think you are speaking to? You may be my husband's sister, but I am your queen! You do not tell me what to do! I will speak to whomever I please, however I please!" The queen then stormed off in a huff.

Two nights before the wedding, Cypros and Salome invited the king to dine with them. After the meal, Cypros dismissed the servants and sat down at a triclinium, staring at her son. The three Roman lectus' that made up the triclinium were positioned in a U-shape around a small square table, adorned with wine and fruit. All three sat adjacent to one another, with Herod being seated in the middle.

"Alright mother..." he said, realizing she was up to something. "What is it? Obviously, you did not invite me here merely to have a pleasant meal."

"Are you completely blind?" Cypros asked candidly.

"What are you talking about?" he chuckled.

"Princess Miriam," Salome elaborated, "Have you not noticed?"

Herod shrugged. "Noticed what?"

Cypros stared at him and shook her head. "She no longer eats with the rest of us."

"She has not been feeling well," Herod explained nonchalantly.

"Is that what she told you?" Salome sneered. Getting up, she strolled over to the terrace.

"Have you not noticed her unhappiness?" Cypros asked. "She is two days away from her wedding, and she's miserable."

Herod stared at his mother narrow-eyed. "What are you saying? Does she not wish to marry me?"

"No Brother..." Salome murmured sarcastically as she swished her wine around in her cup. "We are saying your first wife hates your second." From his blank stare, she could tell he was clueless. Salome rolled her eyes and turned her cup to her head.

"Do you not hear how Doris speaks to her?" Cypros questioned.

Herod shrugged it off and chuckled. "So Doris is jealous; she'll get over it."

"Will she?" Salome muttered under her breath.

Herod stood up and poured himself another cup of wine. "I will see to it that she is civil, but I cannot force one wife to like the other." Cypros folded her arms and stared at him. Herod shrugged. "What? What would you have me do?"

Cypros glanced at her daughter, but Salome promptly turned away and started sipping her wine. Seeing that the task was left to her, Cypros put down her cup and with a heavy sigh, said coldly, "Get rid of her. Divorce her and send her into exile."

"And do it before you wed the Princess," Salome hissed contemptuously.

"What?" Herod laughed. "You jest?" Neither woman was laughing. Realizing they were serious, his smile faded. "You want me to divorce my wife and abandon my son? Days before my wedding?" Glaring at them, he grunted, "You've both gone mad!" Angry, he slammed down his cup and headed for the door.

"She is a thorn in your side, Brother!" Salome called after him. "Can you not see that?"

Herod halted and turned to her. "Is my son also a thorn!"

Salome looked at her mother as she got up. "Antipater is your son, but..." trying to select her words carefully, Cypros said gently as she approached, "he cannot be your heir. Your sons by Princess Miriam are the ones who must inherit the throne."

"They will all be my heirs!" Herod shouted sharply.

"If you want these people to accept you as their king, Princess Miriam is the key!" Cypros insisted. "She is of royal blood and beloved of the people. If they love her, they will love you."

"But if you allow this wench..." Salome started before he interrupted.

"You mean the queen!" Herod snarled.

"If you allow her to continue making the princess' life miserable, you will lose her..." Salome scolded as she approached him.

"And then you will lose the people," Cypros added, stepping before him, "and be forced to spend the rest of your life fighting insurrection! Is that what you want?" Cypros asked.

Herod shifted his gaze from his mother to his sister and back again as he mused. With a heavy sigh, he shook his head. "No. War has cost us too much already. What I want is to go home. But know this...I will not divorce Doris nor will I exile her. Antipater is my firstborn, he will share in the inheritance of his brothers, and if I so chose, he will sit on the throne after me." The women tried to protest, but Herod shut them down. "I will hear no more on the matter! I will speak with the queen about the princess, but like it or not, they both stay! They will just have to find a way to live together."

******

As late evening approached, there was a knock on the queen's door. A dark-skinned maid answered it then came back to the queen; she said timidly, "Forgive the disturbance, my lady."

Brushing her son's curly hair, Doris looked up and asked, "What is it?"

"A visitor."

The maid stepped aside as Princess Miriam entered. Wearing a plain, pale cream dress with a blue veil, she approached and said gently, "We need to talk."

"I have nothing to say to you."

"Well, I have something to say to you." The maid closed the door as Princess Miriam proceeded inside. "In two days, Herod will be husband to us both. For his sake, we must make peace."

Doris turned her attention back to her son, raking the brush through his hair. "Why? So, I can smile while you steal him away?"

"I did not steal him. He chose me," Miriam replied, moving a little closer.

"Because you threw yourself at him like a harlot!"

"Harlot!" Miriam glared at her. If not for her son, she would have slapped her across her face, but instead she came before her and scowled, "I am no harlot! And I did not throw myself at him!"

"Then perhaps you bewitched him with your beauty."

Miriam knelt so she could look Doris in the eyes. "I have done you no wrong. Why do you hate me?"

"Why?" Glaring at her with despising eyes, the queen hissed, "Because he looks at you the way he once looked at me. And now, all he sees is you. I am little more than a shadow." She put down the brush and picked up her son. "You think your royal blood makes you better? Or your beauty? I am a queen, and my son is the king's firstborn—heir to his throne. Long after your beauty fades, I will still be the mother to his heir. What will you be?"

Miriam rested her hands on Doris' knees and said gently, "I will be his second wife, mother of his children, and your sister." Hoping to appease her insecurities, the princess smiled.

Doris leaned down and smiling with her, rested her hands on hers and said, "You will be second..." Her smile fading, she scowled, "But you will never be my sister!! She grabbed Miriam's hands and throwing them off her knees, snarled, "Now get out!!" Miriam got up. Without a word, she headed for the door while Queen Doris screamed after her, "Your sons will never inherit the throne! And in two days, all you have...your wealth, the palace, your kingdoms...they will all belong to me and my son!!"

Miriam walked out and shut the door behind her. Hurrying past the guards, she stopped in the adjoining hallway and burst into tears. After a moment or two, she dried her eyes and hurried off down the hallway, unaware that Herod was standing in the adjacent hallway listening. Coming to speak to the queen, he had arrived, and unbeknown to them, heard much of what was said. He watched Princess Miriam running off then turned a cold gaze towards Doris' door.

****

Early the next morning, there was a knock at the queen's door. Her maid opened it and called to the queen, stepping aside as she approached. Cypros stood at the door with two guards and a maid of her own. "The king wishes to see Antipater," she said, prompting the maid to barge past the queen and fetch the child.

"Alright."

Although she found it unsettling, Doris reluctantly stepped aside and allowed the maid to hand the child to Cypros.

The queen threw a shawl over her shoulder. "I'll come with you."

Cypros, however, looked at one of her guards. He barred the door with his spear as Cypros said indifferently, "Not you. The king wishes to spend time alone with his son."

"Oh." She stood at the doorway watching them leave with Antipater, biting her nails as she pondered why he only wanted to see his son and not her.

******

As the day went on, Herod stood holding his son. "It must be done," Cypros said.

Herod looked at his sister, who added, "For the sake of the kingdom."

Gazing at his son, Herod kissed him on the forehead then with a heavy sigh, looked at Althazar and nodded.

******

By noon, there was another knock at the queen's door. This time, anxiously awaiting the return of her son, she opened it herself. Althazar stood at the doorway with a pair of guards and a scribe who was holding a pair of scrolls and a small vile of hot wax. Unfurling one of the scrolls, the advisor proceeded to read. "By royal order, the king has issued a *Decree of Divorce*. He demands that you sign it, after which you and your son will be exiled to Egypt."

"What!!"

"You will be provided servants and guards, and the rank and provisions of a noblewoman. You and your son will want for nothing."

"I am not going anywhere! Where is my son?" she demanded, but he blocked her pathway. "I want to see the king!"

"The king is otherwise occupied," he replied nonchalantly as he continued to read. "Now, if you fail to comply, your son will be taken away and you will be banished to the furthest reaches of Babylon to live out the rest of your life in poverty. The choice is yours."

"I demand to see my husband!! Where is he?" She pushed past him and started to storm off down the hall, but as she reached the archway leading to the king's chamber, guards blocked her path with crossed spears.

Althazar called to her. "My lady!! The king does not wish to see you! Something about upsetting his future bride!"

Doris halted. Salome, who was leaned up against the arched entrance, swishing her wine around in her cup, looked at her and said smugly, "Told you."

Realizing that Miriam must have brought her complaint to him, she looked at Althazar and screeched, "It's a lie! Whatever she told him, it's a lie!"

"I do not know what you are talking about."

"Princess Miriam! That witch is trying to turn my husband against me! She has filled his head with lies!"

"I assure you…" Althazar said, casually strutting towards her, "Princess Miriam has brought no complaint to the king. Whatever has been done…it is of your own doing."

Desperate, Doris turned back to the guards, demanding, "Let me see my husband! Let me explain! Herod! HEROD!!"

The guards wouldn't budge. Ignoring her pleas, Althazar insisted, "My lady…"

Panicking, Doris pushed past him and turned down the next hall leading to the princess' chamber. "I must speak with Miriam. I can mend this…"

"My lady!"

"I can mend this!" Finding that passage also blocked by guards, Doris burst into tears and screamed in desperation. "Miriam! Sister!!…Forgive me!! Please!!"

"My lady...MY LADY!!" Althazar finally shouted. "It's too late. The king's word is final. You have until noon tomorrow to leave the palace." He held up the two scrolls, one in either hand. "Now, whether you leave a free woman with your son..." indicating the scroll in his right hand, "...or a prisoner bound in chains..." he said, indicating the one on the left, "...is up to you." One of the guards beside him unlatched a heavy iron chain from his hip and held it in his hand. Althazar unfurled the scroll in his right hand, titled *Decree of Divorce,* and gestured to her chambers. "Now, will you sign the king's decree?"

Just before noon the next day, holding her son in her arms, Doris stood by a pillar of the upper hallway overlooking the palace gardens. Lush green vines spotted with white flowers hung from the top of red and gold marble porticoes. Intricate hedges and rows of pristine palm trees wrapped with white silk curtains, bordered the parameter of the extensive lawn. Along the inside were gold urns arrayed with large bouquets of colorful flowers intertwined with red silk ribbons. They stood between bronze fountains lining both sides of the wide path leading to the palace. In the midst of the gardens, hundreds of prestigious guests were seated at tables positioned around a large pond, interspersed with white lilies. As they listened to musicians playing soft melodies on flutes and harps, the guests talked quietly among themselves, commenting on everything from the royal family's extravagant attire to the noticeable absence of King Herod's first wife and child.

"My lady, if you please." Zoltan stood waiting on her with a pair of armed guards, resting their hands on their swords. He gestured towards the entrance.

Tears streaming down her face, Doris handed her son to one of her maids and left the palace—humiliated and broken. As she left, four maidens dressed in red came out bearing the gold posts of a large white canopy. Beneath it, walked Princess Miriam in a Judean-Greek dress of pure white trimmed with gold. Her face was covered beneath a veil, on which sat a gold crown inlaid with rubies.

As Doris left the Samarian palace grounds in a small caravan consisting of a few dozen armed guards, servants and a small chest of gold, Miriam and Herod stood beneath the white canopy. Having said their vows, they exchanged a passionate kiss, and to the adulation of the crowd, emerged husband and wife: King and Queen of Judea.

As fate would have it, the day after the wedding celebrations ended, and the guest had taken their leave, vigorous knocking at the door of his chambers awakened Herod. "What is it?" he rumbled.

As a servant opened the door, Althazar rushed inside and announced, "My king! They are here!!"

"Who's here?" Herod murmured, groggily rubbing his eyes as Miriam shifted from off his chest.

"The Romans! They are here!"

His eyes wide open, Herod sat up and asked, "How many?"

"60, 000!"

A few moments later, King Herod pushed open the decorated shutters and stepped out onto the balcony of his throne room overlooking the courtyard. A crown on his head, golden rings around the curls of his hair, sporting a thick beard, and dressed in a white tunic overlaid with a royal blue and white striped robe, he peered out with Althazar at his side. Before him sat the Roman general and 30 of his commanders on horseback.

Seated on a black stallion, arrayed in a bronze breastplate, manica and greaves, a black robe and a formidable helmet with black plumes, the general looked up and called, "King Herod! General Antony sends his regards and a gift." He alluded to a Roman foot soldier leading a white stallion into the courtyard. He was followed by a pair of servants carrying a large chest, which they placed down at the foot of the steps beneath the king's balcony. They opened it, revealing a golden breastplate and armor resting on a scarlet robe trimmed with gold buckles, and a helmet crowned with a white horse tail.

"Outstanding!" Herod exclaimed, grinning. "I will be sure to express my gratitude to him in person."

Removing his helmet, the general announced, "I am General Sosius, and I am here to offer you the services of eleven legions of Rome." The general gestured to the sea of red cloaks and gleaming bronze and iron armor spread out through the streets leading all the way up to the hills.

A smile curling on the king's lips, he announced, "Have your men rested, General. In three days, we march on Jerusalem."

31

KILL THEM ALL

When King Antigonus' spies reported that a large Roman contingent had been spotted heading for Galilee, he had sent an urgent message to Prince Pacorus imploring the Parthians to come to his aid. Almost a month had passed and he had received no reply. Now, with new reports that the Romans had joined forces with Herod's army and were preparing to march on Jerusalem, the king was in a panic. His only hope of defeating the allied armies was if the Parthians reached Jerusalem before his enemy arrived. One early afternoon, a small Parthian party arrived. Among them, a messenger hurried inside, demanding to see the king. "At last!" Antigonus muttered under his breath, glancing at Rabbi Babas and his sons as they watched the messenger approach the throne.

"Great King Antigonus! King Orodes sends you his greetings."

"Yes, yes..." Antigonus muttered with a dismissive wave. "Where is the Prince? Where is his army?"

The messenger lowered his eyes and handed him a sealed scroll. "Prince Pacorus led a campaign to capture Syria from the Romans. He met the Roman general, Ventidius, on the battlefield, but the Romans held the higher ground and the prince was unaware that the general had laid a snare for his army. Our horsemen were at the front, driving the army uphill to meet the enemy..."

"Spare me the details. Where is Prince Pacorus?" Antigonus demanded.

"That is what I am trying to tell you, my lord. The battle was lost. Our men were defeated; many fell on the battlefield that day. Among them...was Prince Pacorus."

The king's heart sank. He got up, deeply troubled. He had not just lost a friend, but his closest ally. He looked at the messenger and asked, "So, there are no reinforcements coming?"

Disappointed that reinforcements seemed to be his only concern, the messenger replied, "No. The king cannot afford to risk further loss of our troops when our defenses are so weakened."

"Then we are on our own," Zahid remarked, as he contemplated his options.

"Silence!" King Antigonus snapped, shifting his gaze from Zahid to the messenger. Pushing aside his despondence, he said solemnly, "Convey my deepest regrets to your king. He has lost a son, and I, a brother. My guards will escort you out, and my servants will send you on your way with provision and a gift for your king."

The messenger bowed and followed the guards out. The moment he left, Babas demanded, "What are we to do? Who will defend us now?"

His brow furrowed as he peered out over the city, King Antigonus glanced at Hiam and ordered, "Send out patrols throughout the city and the surrounding hills. Gather every able man and boy that can hold a weapon—drag them from their homes, if needed, and then barricade the gates. Come morning, I want all who are not my enemy defending our walls!" Babas shot his sons a cynical glance as Antigonus looked around his court and yelled belligerently, "I will NOT GIVE HEROD THIS CITY!!"

****

Early the next morning, Jerusalem was awakened to several blasts of shofars sounding from one watchtower to the next. Guards and soldiers went scrambling to their posts, and putting the city in high alert.

Equally startled, King Antigonus stumbled out of bed just as Zahid, followed by several guards, burst through his doors and announced, "My king, they are here!"

With his servants hurriedly following behind, dressing him in his armor, King Antigonus hurried out onto the citadel wall where two of his commanders were already directing the guards to their post. Others were directing the soldiers on the city wall and around the temple.

Just as Antigonus reached the watchtower, a projectile came sailing through the air, smashing into it. A handful of guards tried to shield him. As they moved their shields, the king saw what it was...Commander Pappus' rotting head—King Herod had dried it in the sun, for just this occasion.

Several other severed heads came flying over the wall too, smashing into various parts of the city. The heads of Pappus' army and staunch supporters of King Antigonus soon littered the streets, driving fear into the city's occupants.

Seated on his new horse outside the gates, arrayed in his new armor and scarlet robe, Herod shouted up, "Now that I have your attention...People of Jerusalem! Hear me!! I stood here once before offering you terms of peace. You chose to mock me! So now I stand here with an ultimatum! Surrender! Turn that traitor,

Antigonus over to me and receive me as your king, and you shall live! Refuse me...and you will die!!"

"Half-Jew!!" Antigonus yelled from the wall. "You are no king of ours! You are not even of noble birth!! Look at him," he turned his attention to the crowd of soldiers and civilians on the wall, defending the city, "He is just a sewer-rat who crawled up from the gutter, and now thinks he can call himself our king!" Turning back to Herod, he shouted, "The people have chosen! I am their king! And we will never surrender!!"

"Then you will die!!" Herod's threat silenced them.

Destroyer landed on the highest tower of the citadel. Ready for battle, he was dressed in heavy, battle-worn armor, a crown-like helmet with nine jagged spires and a black leathery robe blowing between his large black wings. Invisible to the eyes of men, he watched and listened.

"Look at what stands before you!!" Herod shouted. King Antigonus and all the city's defenses glared at the vast army of Romans and Jews that surrounded them. 60,000 Romans and 40,000 Jews armed with siege ramps, catapults and every conceivable weapon, awaiting the command to fight. "Before this day ends, Jerusalem will be mine! And all who oppose me will be dead! So, this is your last chance! Hand over the usurper and open the gates!!"

After a moment of deliberation, the Jews on the wall began to chant, "King Antigonus! King Antigonus! King Antigonus!"

Glaring at them, Herod drew his sword and scowled, "So be it!!" As his sword came down, the catapults were released. Great boulders and huge rocks went flying, smashing into the walls, homes and market stalls, crumpling stones and crushing all who fell in their path. Antigonus' troops fired a volley of arrows, impaling hundreds, but the Romans used their shield formation to form a wall as they advanced. Their archers fired back until the sky was darkened with clouds of deadly projectiles crossing back and forth.

Once the catapults breached the wall, Herod signaled the commanders with siege ramps to advance; and General Sosius *(arrayed in a white robe and a white plumed helmet)* signaled the Roman commanders leading the infantry to attack. The Romans moved in formation using their shields to protect themselves and those pushing the siege ramps, allowing them to advance on the city while arrows rained down on both sides of the wall. Men fell by the hundreds, and by the time the siege ramps and ladders were up against the walls, men were dying by the thousands.

The Romans were relentless, scaling up the siege ramps, dozens at a time. Antigonus' men hurled down clay jars filled with oil and wine at them while archers set them ablaze with flaming arrows. Screaming, the soldiers scrambled as they burned.

Some, battling through a barrage of arrows, made it to the top of the wall, while others poured in where the wall had been breached by the catapults, only to be met with fierce resistance.

Dividing his troops under various commanders, Herod and General Sosius had deliberately focused their attack on the western wall, so that Antigonus' troops wouldn't notice Sohemus leading his men to where the defenses were weakest—the temple. Using ladders, they scaled the temple wall; hundreds of Roman soldiers followed.

The moment his feet hit the ground, Sohemus drew his long, curved sword and shield, and charged towards the rebel guards. Built like an ox, with the quickness and ferocity of a bear, Sohemus used his shield and barreled through them, knocking several off the wall. Screaming, they plummeted to the courtyard below where their bones were broken and their skulls smashed on the stone floor. With a burst of rage, Sohemus surged towards the enemy, slashing and hacking his way through with such brutality, a Roman commander named Lucius, fighting along side him, remarked, "You fight like a Roman!"

Sohemus laughed. "I almost take that as a complement!" The two stood back to back, fighting off rebels whose blue sashes and light soft leather breastplates made them easy to distinguish from Herod's men in red sashes and thick tempered hide armor.

Despite a fervent effort to fend them off, the Romans were too quick and too many; they swarmed the temple like ants. The ill-equipped guards stood little chance against them. By the time King Antigonus looked across and realized what was happening, calling for reinforcements, every guard on the temple wall was dead. The city was breached. Thousands of Romans stormed the temple slaughtering the priests, and then they started killing those who had taken refuge there.

When Antigonus saw that the Romans had breached the temple, he took refuge in the citadel while the Romans broke down the temple's inner gates and spilled out into the streets, slaughtering all they came across.

The catapults ceased, giving way to the timed thump of battering rams. With the city's defenses under attack from both sides of the wall, it didn't take long for the thick wooden gates to begin to crack.

Sending his uncle—Joseph, and Hippicus to attack from the north side of the city, Herod centered his attack on the south. He glanced at Costobarus and Zoltan, and ordered, "Take your men and guard all the gates. No-one leaves the city! Neither rich nor poor! And Commanders...if you see any kin of the royal family...kill them!" Zoltan nodded, but somewhat surprised by the king's command, Costobarus stared at Herod for a moment, before riding off.

The southern gates began to buckle. His eyes blazing like fire, *Destroyer* stretched out his giant black wings and took to the air, bellowing a roar that blasted across the plains like a strong gust of wind. The gates came crashing down. The army filled with bloodlust, Herod lifted his sword and yelled, "FORWARD!!"

He and General Sosius led the charge inside, surging through the entrance with an army tens of thousands strong—all hungering to spill blood. And riding off in opposite directions, Costobarus and Zoltan sent their troops to seal off all the exits, preventing anyone from escaping.

Worried that if the Romans plundered the Temple of God, the people would never accept him as their king, upon entering the city, Herod led a group of his men toward the temple. He left General Sosius to lead the assault on the rest of the city. With *Destroyer* hovering over them, directing his demons to spread havoc across the city, the moment King Herod was out of sight, General Sosius raised his sword and raged, "KILL THEM ALL!!!"

Being driven by a lust for blood, the Romans went through the streets and houses on a brutal rampage, plundering the city and killing everyone not wearing the red sash and armor of Herod's army. Men, women and children—from the old to the young—they spared no-one. They slaughtered until blood covered every wall and ran through the streets like a stream amidst piles of corpses. General Sosius was the most brutal. Jumping down off his horse, he picked up a second sword and walked through the streets, wantonly butchering everyone he came across. Within minutes, his armor, white robe and the plumes of his helmet were dripping with blood.

When King Antigonus stared out from the safety of the citadel. He was horrified. "They are slaughtering everyone!"

When Zahid looked out and saw bodies piling up in the streets for miles in every direction, he stumbled back muttering, "So many dead." He looked at the king. Terrified, he tore off his blue sash and ran off. Antigonus called after him, but it was no use. Even the servants started to abandon their stations.

Antigonus sent for Itiel. The butler came running in. "Yes, my king."

"Take some guards through the back streets and get Babas and his family out of the city. If Herod takes Jerusalem, I will need them to help me reclaim the throne."

"Yes, my lord." Itiel nodded and hurried out.

Spotting the rogue king peering out, General Sosius looked up and bellowed, "Antigonus! You coward!! See the wrath you have brought on your people!!" Overturning a cart, and finding a handful of people cowering beneath it, the general looked up at the king and with a grimace, slaughtered them before him.

Unable to watch anymore, the rebel king turned away, and looking at his men, murmured, "This isn't what I wanted."

****

Reveling in the brutal carnage, *Destroyer* hovered over the city, roaring with laughter, but it ended abruptly when the archangel—Michael, came flying at him like a spear. He ploughed headfirst into the demon with such speed, *Destroyer* didn't realize what happened until Michael careened him into the roof of a building hundreds of feet down the road. A young child— who had been hiding inside—peered out. From the midst of a cloud of falling rubble and debris, the archangel and demon-lord, drew their weapons.

Grasping his massive sword, Michael snarled, "I told you to stay away from Jerusalem!! Did you not hear me!!" He lunged at the demon, slashing at him with a swift, powerful blow. *Destroyer* met it with an equally powerful block by crossing a pair of large curved swords. The clash of their weapons sent tremors through the ground and lightning rippling through the clouds visible through the hole above them.

Michael suddenly broke the hold, bashing *Destroyer* across the face with his shield. As the demon staggered back, Michael lashed at him with a fury of swift blows. *Destroyer* managed to block and kick the archangel back and snarled, "If you have come to save the city...you're too late!"

He swung at the archangel. Michael ducked and veered out the way. Spinning and blocking him, he growled, "I did not come to save them from Herod, I came to save them from you!!"

32

WARFARE

After battling his way into the temple, Herod was relieved to find that Sohemus had managed to maintain command of the Romans and prevent them from looting it, but he was appalled at the great number of civilians that lay dead. Ordering them to stop fighting, Herod walked through the courtyard, examining the bodies scattered over the ground. Aside from the guards, most were ordinary citizens. "What is this?" he asked in dismay. "Women! Children! Priests!! They are not even armed!" He looked at Sohemus. "These people came here to take refuge, and you let them slaughter them all like dogs!"

"You said all who oppose you would die," Sohemus answered.

"Women and children!" Herod glared at him bewildered. "I was talking about the men, you fool!!"

Sohemus tried to justify himself, but he couldn't find the words. Looking at them now, he realized they had shed innocent blood, but at the time, he—like the rest of them—only wanted vengeance and blood. Infuriated, Herod looked at the Romans. "This ends! From now on, you only put down those with weapons!" He called to one of his men and ordered, "Find General Sosius!"

Michael countered *Destroyer's* attack with several powerful swings, driving the demon back. Both seemed unaware that the young boy was watching, but as the battle between them ensued, the war worsened. The Roman general continued his ruthless rampage, slaughtering everyone he came across.

Desperately attempting to escape, Zahid made his way out into the streets. He managed to evade the Romans by ducking behind rubble and hiding amidst the dead, but there was no way he could escape the city without running into his enemy. Armed or unarmed, they weren't taking prisoners. There was only one way he was going to escape. He searched among the dead, hiding in the shadows until he came across one of Herod's dead soldiers. Dragging him behind a smashed market stall, Zahid emerged dressed as one of them. He looked around, then picking up the dead soldier's sword, stepped out into the street and nervously started moving towards an opening in the wall.

As he turned the corner, he ran into a group of Romans looking for rebel forces. Terrified, Zahid halted, wondering if they realized he wasn't one of them; but upon seeing the armor and red sash, they ignored him. His heart pounding, he nodded and turned the other way, only to run into Antigonus' rebel soldiers.

One of the rebels ran towards him, lifting his sword to attack, but when he recognized Zahid, he halted. "I know you!" he exclaimed. Zahid looked at him. Panicking, he looked back at the Romans. "You are one of..." Before the soldier could finish his sentence, Zahid slashed his sword across his throat, silencing him. Blood pouring from his neck, the guard went down with a look of bewilderment. He couldn't understand why one of their own men was dressed as their enemy, nor would he be able to reveal it. Three others suddenly came running towards him. Zahid lifted his sword and planted his feet, but there were too many, and being the coward that he was, he wasn't about to get himself killed by his own men. Staggering back and preparing to run, he suddenly found himself surrounded by Romans.

Running in from behind, they engaged the rebels, allowing him to slowly back away unnoticed and head for the wall. With one last look around, Zahid slipped out through the opening just as General Sosius came storming through.

****

Furious blow after blow, and weapons clashing, shook the ground and atmosphere. Michael skillfully fought against the demon-lord until *Destroyer* managed to knock his sword from his hand, and then the helmet from his head. He charged at him with both swords, but the archangel blocked and buffeted him with his shield, landing several sharp elbows to his face before sending *Destroyer* careening into the floor with a powerful uppercut.

The demon crashed into the ground, churning up rock, dirt and stone as he slid. By the time he came to a skidding stop, Michael had landed beside him. He grabbed the demon by the throat, but as he lifted him, *Destroyer* knocked him back with an uppercut. Michael landed with a heavy thud. When he got back on his feet, *Destroyer* was running at him. He slashed both swords across his throat. The archangel veered back, narrowly escaping the sharp edge of the blade. As the blades separated, Michael ducked under *Destroyer's* arms. He grabbed his wrists and twisted, forcing the demon to drop the weapons, before he kicked him clear across the room and sent him crashing into the wall. *Destroyer* returned glaring at him. Reaching around to his back, he plucked a pair of heavy axes tucked beneath his wings. Spreading his wings, he leapt through the air and came down on the spot where Michael was standing. The archangel darted and rolled out of the way, then jumped to his feet, fighting and blocking the demon's savage attack.

****

Seeing the Roman brutality spreading throughout the city, and realizing they had lost the war, townspeople and even rebel soldiers started scrambling for the gates and openings in the walls; they were met by King Herod's troops, who herded them back with spears and swords. Zoltan had taken a group of men and spread them out across the northern gates while Costobarus spread his men across the east and west.

Disguised as townspeople, Itiel and the small contingent of guards surrounding Babas and his family were pushing their way through the crowd gathered near one of the gates. They were desperately trying to get out, but as mayhem broke out, Babas fell victim to a spear.

Caught in the throng of the panicking crowd, Itiel's guards started cutting down those blocking their path until they managed to get all the way to the gate. They were met by several of Herod's men with spears and their commander on his horse, threatening, "Get back!! All of you!!"

Recognizing the man on the horse, Itiel called to him. "Costobarus!! Commander! You know me! Itiel, I was butler in the palace!"

"And now you serve the usurper!" Costobarus growled. "Get back with the others, traitor!"

"Wait! Please Commander, let me speak with you! I beg you!" Itiel held out his hand to Malachi. Though grieving over his father, he handed the butler a pouch. Itiel then made his way to the commander. "Here." He discretely handed it to Costobarus. "There is plenty more," Itiel said, "Just let us leave."

The commander opened the pouch. Upon seeing it filled with gold coins, he looked down at him and asked, "Where did you get this?"

Itiel gestured to Babas. "Do you recognize him?"

Costobarus looked at Babas' face as he lay lifeless in his son's arms. "Yes."

"Then you know the wealth he possessed and the power his name commanded?"

"And now he is dead."

"Yet, his sons live. Set them free and they will be in your debt."

Costobarus hissed, "I have orders to kill them."

"Dead, they are martyrs; alive, they are allies," Itiel impressed. "Surely, a man like you can see the value in..."

Costobarus drew his sword and holding it to Itiel's throat, snarled, "What do you know of me? I serve King Herod!..." He glared at the trembling butler's, peering up at him doe-eyed. "But not for long," he murmured. Costobarus lifted his sword and signalled two of his men, ordering, "Bring them."

The soldiers headed over to Babas' family, while Itiel gestured for them to come. "Thank you," he said, looking up at the commander.

"Leave him," Costobarus ordered, pointing to Babas as Malachi and his brother started to lift their father.

"But he is their father," Itiel protested.

Costobarus leaned down and snarled, "I'm already risking my life. I will not leave a trail of blood for their enemy to follow to my gate. Now leave him...or they can all stay!"

Dismayed, Itiel looked at Malachi and shook his head. Reluctantly, they laid Babas back down and grabbing their families, hurried towards him as the soldier pushed them through the crowd.

Meanwhile, Costobarus called one of his trusted guards and quietly ordered, "Take these men to my estate and keep them out of sight until I arrive tomorrow." The guard nodded and ushered them towards the gate.

The moment the soldiers allowed them through the gate, the crowd tried to push through behind them. Costobarus' men started cutting them down.

Knowing that his men would not question his orders, once Babas' family was through the gate, the commander ordered his men to pull back and then shouted, "Burn them all!"

The crowd immediately began to scream and panic. The sons of Babas and their families were hidden in carts and driven off. They left behind the haunting shrills of the crowd screaming and trampling one another, trying to escape as 200 archers up on the wall penned them in and sprayed them with several volleys of burning arrows, setting blaze to everyone and everything in sight. Not one soul was left alive to speak of the commander's betrayal.

33

BLOOD AND SAND

All over the city, people started laying down their weapons and surrendering, hoping to find mercy—they found none. Having the intention of driving fear into their king, General Sosius had his men line up a group of prisoners and force them to their knees. Among them were the widower, Anna, and a devout man named Simeon. General Sosius stood over a young woman and looking up at the citadel, yelled, "Antigonus!! The hand of Rome is upon your throat!! You coward!!" He raised his sword.

Suddenly, the gate of the citadel opened. "STOP!!" King Antigonus stepped out through the gate and dropped his sword. "It's me you want."

****

After being hurled through a wall, *Destroyer* emerged with a roar. Enraged, he opened his fist.

Michael watched as long iron darts extended from tips of his scaled iron gloves. With a flick of his wrists, the darts flew towards Michael like a salvo of arrows, one then the other. With no time to fetch his shield, Michael used his gold manicas to deflect each projectile with lightning speed. The young boy, still watching from the rubble, shifted. A rock by his foot tumbled down. *Destroyer* looked at Michael and proclaimed, "You think you can protect these insects from me? I am *THE DESTROYER!!* I am everywhere! I lay waste to empires, consume nations and slaughter the innocent!" He suddenly shifted his gaze to the boy and shot a salvo of darts in his direction. The archangel dove in front of the boy, using his wings to shield him. He flinched as the darts hit his giant wings. Yet, cradled in a luminescent glow of light flowing through his feathers, and engulfed in an overwhelming sense of peace, the child looked up unafraid. Michael looked down at him with his golden eyes, smiled and said, "Go." The little boy ran off, glancing back at the archangel as Michael spread his wings, shielding him from the flying darts.

Seeing a pair of demons holding down the child's angel, Michael pulled a pair of gold hilted daggers from his belt and hurled them, simultaneously taking out both demons. He then clenched his fists and shook his wings. *Destroyer* watched as the darts fell to the ground. His smile fading, the archangel turned around and looked at the demon-lord. "We're done here."

Running towards him, Michael picked up his sword and shield. Knocking away several short axe-like weapons *Destroyer* hurled at him as he spread his wings, he took to the air, raising his sword.

"NOW!!" *Destroyer* shouted. Hundreds of demons suddenly descended with a massive heavy net, dropping it on top of Michael, pinning him to the ground with a thunderous thud.

****

The general raised his hand and ordered, "Halt!!" The soldiers around him immediately stopped fighting. Lowering his sword, he strutted towards the king.

"I surrender. I beg you…spare my people!"

General Sosius looked down on him and asked, "You beg me?"

"Yes, I'm begging you," the king said quietly.

The Roman general strutted around him, staring at him curiously. He punched him in the gut then kicked him in the back of the leg. As the king dropped to his knees, Sosius struck him across the face and jeered, "So this is the mighty King Antigonus! The man who took the throne and held Jerusalem captive for three years! Now look at him...begging for mercy! You know what I think? I think he whines like a woman!" He grabbed the king by the hair and yanked back his head. "So, I think we should call him...Princess Antigona!" General Sosius and the others roared with laughter, even more so when he cracked the king across the face with his knee, knocking him to the ground.

While Antigonus staggered to get up, General Sosius went and stood over a male prisoner and sneered, "Beg me again, princess!"

Humiliated, King Antigonus quietly begged, "Spare my people."

General Sosius suddenly thrust his sword through the prisoner's back and moved to the next. "What was that Antigona? I didn't hear you?"

"I said, I beg you to spare my people!" the king shouted.

"Louder!!" General Sosius ran his sword through the prisoner before him and moved onto the next.

****

The archangel struggled to break free, but there were too many demons holding him down. His eyes aglow, he tried to blast them with fire, but *Destroyer* and dozens of others surrounded him with a wall of shields, while one of the demons slapped an iron mask on his face, extinguishing the flames. Disarming him, they cuffed a pair of shackles on his arms, each with dozens of long iron chains attached. Hundreds of demons were pulling on them, wrenching his arms apart so that he couldn't move.

With a smug grin on his gnarled face, and shrouded in dust, *Destroyer* landed on the rubble before Michael and scoffed, "Did you really think I would come alone?" His smile fading and his black eyes glassing over as he watched the archangel struggle to break free, the demon-lord drew his large curved sword. "Look at what I have wrought...tell me, Commander of God's army, where is He who will save you from me?"

Though Michael struggled to break free of the chains, there were too many demons restraining him.

****

"PLEASE! STOP! I'M BEGGING YOU!!" Antigonus shrieked as the Roman general slaughtered another prisoner.

"Well, that's more like it," General Sosius sneered, "But I don't think..." He looked down at the prisoner and asked, "What's your name?"

Frightened, the man looked at King Antigonus and answered, "Simeon."

"I don't think Simeon heard you!"

Sobbing, Antigonus shouted, "What do you want from me!"

"I want all Jerusalem to hear you beg!! You pathetic worm! And then I'm going to make you watch as I slaughter them!!"

The general lifted his sword over Simeon's neck, but hearing what sounded like muttering coming from him, he halted and listened.

"Lord, God of our fathers, protect this city and deliver us from the hand of the destroyer." Simeon was praying. The general looked down at him, amused.

Anna, who was next in line, also started to pray, *"Oh Lord, my God, deliver us from evil this day and stay the hand of the destroyer."*

"Listen to this!" he called to his men. "They're praying! They think their God is going to save them?" General Sosius jeered as he burst into laughter and lifted his sword.

"STOP!!" Herod yelled. The general halted with his sword hovering over Simeon's neck.

****

"When I am done with you, I will destroy this city," *Destroyer* taunted, leaning in closer to Michael's ear. "No Jerusalem! No Promise! No Savior!" A sudden ray of light beamed through the roof, enveloping Michael. The archangel basked in its warmth as *Destroyer* continued to threaten, "Mankind will be lost, and the earth will be..."

The mask suddenly fell off the archangel's face. *Destroyer* stared at him wide-eyed. Michael growled, "The earth is the Lord's! Both now and forever!!" He suddenly head-butted the demon-lord, cracking him hard enough on the skull to knock him off his feet. Clenching his fist and wrenching his arms towards his chest, Michael let out a powerful roar. The chains shattered and the demons tugging on them went tumbling back. The archangel flew up into the air and landed with his fist pounding the ground, sending the demons flying in every direction as he levelled the building on top of them, and stated, "Do you not know, the prayer of one will chase 1000, and two will put 10,000 demons to flight!"

In a fit of rage, *Destroyer* scrambled to his feet and ran at him. A stream of fire blazed from Michael's eyes, bringing the demon to a halt as the flames burned his face. Destroyer cried out as his helmet melted onto his skin. Smoke rising from the demon's charred face, Michael grabbed him by the throat, picked him up, and growled, "Tell your master, the Lord Almighty says...his days are numbered!" He tossed *Destroyer* up and punched him with such immense force, he sent the demon-lord hurtling back into the Dark Realm. His eyes aglow, Michael turned and looked at the others; they scattered into the darkness like roaches. Picking up his helmet, sword and shield, the archangel ascended. He stopped to look over the city as demons everywhere began to descend back into the earth. Spreading his wings, Michael shot back up into the sky and disappeared.

****

"What do you think you are doing?" King Herod demanded, marching towards General Sosius.

The general slowly lowered his sword. Though he was ruthless and sadistic, now that the *destroying spirit* had been dispelled, his sense of reason began to return. He looked down at the unarmed prisoners and shrugged, "Winning the war for you."

"Our enemy has surrendered: the war is already won!" Herod replied, standing face to face with him. "I came here to win back the city, not massacre it! So, unless you intend to leave me the king of blood and sand, order your men to stand down!"

Only now realizing that he was drenched in blood, the general looked around at the horrific carnage. There were dead prisoners at his feet and bodies piled, one on top of the other, in every direction. General Sosius looked across at one of his commanders and soberly gave the order, "Stand down!" The commander gave the signal, and at the blast of several ram's horns travelling throughout the city, the Romans stopped fighting. The war was at an end.

Glancing at the defeated king on his knees, Herod turned to his troops and proclaimed, "The war is over! JERUSALEM IS OURS!"

****

In the darkness, *Destroyer's shrieks* trailing across the obsidian sky came to a crashing end as he smashed through the rock wall of Lucifer's fortress. He rolled across the floor amidst rock and debris before landing at the foot of the steps leading to his master's throne. Breathing a heavy sigh of disappointment, the Prince of Darkness looked down at him with disgust.

AMYZONN KNIGHT

34

GOAT PIE

At the end of the day, while prisoners were being rounded up and the dead cleared away, as Herod started making his way to the palace, his uncle Joseph called to him, "My lord!" Herod looked back. Upon seeing his uncle approaching him with something or someone wrapped in a robe and slung over a horse, Herod halted. A couple of men brought the body down and laid it on the ground before the king. Tears filling his eyes, his first thought was his last surviving brother. "Pheroras?" Fear wrenching his heart, he reached down and lifted the robe. It was Hippicus, lying dead.

"An arrow went through his chest," Joseph explained sadly.

Falling to his knees, Herod closed his eyes. "Hippicus, my brother!" He lifted his head and began to wail. As close to him as any brother, his dearest friend was dead, and his victory, bittersweet.

Citizens were allowed two days to bury their dead, and thousands of slaves were consigned to remove the blood and rubble from the streets, while workers—under the supervision of Pheroras—began repairs on the wall.

Herod had assigned the third day to be that of his coronation, and had the High Priest officially declare him King of the Jews. That day, many who had been staunch supporters of Herod throughout his campaign, gathered in the temple. Herod stood out in the palace courtyard and looked around. Before being hit with all the excitement, he just wanted to take a moment and breathe it all in.

"Are you all right, my love?" Miriam asked, squeezing his hand.

Herod nodded. "I'm just taking it in. It's been three years since we were forced to flee this palace. I left here a tetrarch and return a king." He kissed her hand and smiled muttering, "It's good to be home."

His smile slowly fading, Miriam knew what was troubling him. "None of them are here to see your day of glory."

Herod's gaze lowered into despair. "Phasael, Seth and Hippicus—he was closer to me than a brother. We have been friends since childhood. He and I were always playing tricks on Phasael. I remember this one time when mother had made his favorite meal—goat pie with spiced honey and roasted corn. The pie had just come out of the stone-oven. Phasael put it on the table in the courtyard to cool, and sat there watching it. We took his favorite head-wrap—a red one with blue lines—Hippicus tied it around the head of one of the dogs while I put a piece of meat on a long string and tied it to the tail of one of the palace cats. I chased the cat into the courtyard then Hippicus sent the dog in after it. When my brother saw the dog chasing the cat while wearing his head-wrap, he was livid. He took off after it. The dog chased the cat up into a tree. Phasael found the dog still wearing his head-wrap, trying to eat the meat dangling from the cat's tail. He didn't give a second thought to that pie, until he got that head-wrap. By the time he ran back to the courtyard, the pie was gone. Hippicus and I climbed up the highest tower and we ate that goat pie..." Both he and Miriam began to laugh. "I can still hear him stomping around the yard yelling, 'Herod! Hippicus! I'm going to kill you!' It was the best pie we ever tasted." They both chuckled, but soon Herod's laughter faded; his gaze lowered, replaced with a heavy sigh. "They were my closest friends. I don't know what I will do without them."

Miriam caressed his neck and with a gentle smile, said, "They would have been proud of you, my love."

Herod nodded and smiled. "That, they would."

With a passionate kiss, she said warmly, "Then go...make them proud."

35

PROMISES AND LIES

Lucifer watched from the shadows as Herod sat while Ananelus—the newly appointed High Priest—anointed his head with oil and placed a decorative gold crown on his head. The High Priest declared, "People of Judea, by Divine appointment of God and Rome, behold our liberator and king...KING HEROD THE GREAT!"

A resounding eruption of cheers echoed through the temple and the surrounding streets all the way to the palace, though not all shared the sentiment. Princess Alexandra watched him, praying that God would strike him down where he stood, while her son watched in dismay as his crown was being given to the man who had promised to make *him* king. At Herod's insistence, King Antigonus was forced to witness the Half-Jew's coronation on his knees, bound in Roman chains and muzzled like a dog.

Raising his hands to quiet the crowd, King Herod stepped forward and addressed the people of Jerusalem. "For the last 30 years, this city has known only death and war. Well, today...that war ends! This day marks the beginning of a new era! It marks the end of one dynasty, and the beginning of another..."

The king may have been saying one thing, but his mind was pouring over many others:

Although many were hailing him as king, throughout Jerusalem there were some who did not see him as their liberator. His appointment as king instead of the young Jewish prince, particularly after massacring almost a third of the city, had only added insult to injury. They hated him even more, but fearing the heavy Roman presence still patrolling the streets, they had shown their distain the only way they could.

After burying Hippicus and the remains of his brothers in the tomb of his father, King Herod led a parade of royal chariots through the streets in a victorious procession. Upon hearing roaring cheers, Herod lifted his hand and waved—until he realized, the cheers were not for him. Nor were they for the defeated usurper being paraded behind them in a cage, surrounded by a heavily armed Roman escort.

Much of the crowd was chanting, "ARIS! ARIS! ARIS!!"

The more they chanted his name, the more people joined in, until those chanting his name drowned out those chanting, "King Herod!" The king's smile faded. He lowered his hand and looked back at the prince riding in the carriage behind him. Dressed in a white and gold robe—marvelling at the crowd's adulation, Prince Aris waved, prompting them to chant his name even louder. Herod's eye turned cold, warming only temporarily when Queen Miriam squeezed his hand.

****

"We can look forward to an era of hope...." he continued, looking over the crowd.

****

During a feast being held in the new king's honor, King Herod sat on his throne—somber. Despite the aroma of roasted lamb stuffed with figs filling the halls, and musicians playing while dancers skillfully twirled colorful silk scarves, the moment was bittersweet. It was far from what he imagined. No revelry or laughter could drown out the rumble of protestors gathered at the gates, belligerently shouting, "We want Antigonus! Death to the Half-Jew!!" Dancers could not quash the *awful images of his murdered brothers. And no amount of music could sooth his grief or quell his raging anger against those who had brought such misery on his family.*

****

"For I shall rule Judea with peace and justice...." Herod articulated, while thinking about the orders he had given Sohemus and Costobarus.

****

At his command, Sohemus and Costobarus plundered the gold of those loyal to King Antigonus, using it to pay the Romans.

****

"Take no retribution on those who denied me power...."

****

Also at his command, his men lined up 45 prominent leaders who supported the rebel king and slaughtered them to drive fear into all those who opposed him.

****

"Mine, shall be a hand of mercy...

****

With Sohemus and General Sosius standing at the entrance of the dungeon, King Herod peered down at Antigonus, chained to a wooden post.

"If you have come to gloat, Half-Jew, then perhaps you should listen to the people..." Antigonus murmured, chuckling as he listened to protestors calling his name. "It is my name they call, not yours."

"I have not come to gloat! I have come to avenge my brothers!" Herod snarled. He drew his sword and held the blade to his throat.

"I did not kill your brothers," Antigonus replied. "Seth was already dead, when I found him!"

"By your orders!!" Enraged, Herod grabbed his hair and yanked back Antigonus' head. Shunting the blade to his throat, he growled, "Where is his head?"

Defiantly, Antigonus hissed, "Kill me and you'll never find it!"

"That is just the answer I was hoping for. Philoneus!" Herod released him and looked across the room. A large man whose scars and hard lines gave him a particularly sinister appearance, stepped out of the shadows holding a red-hot dagger. He came and stood over him. Cracking his neck, he looked down and grimaced.

Antigonus' agonizing screams were not heard over the loud music, but when his screams finally died down, wincing, he shrieked, "It's buried in the tomb of my father!!"

Philoneus stepped back and stuck the dagger back into the flames. King Herod nodded at Sohemus. He called one of his guards and sent him off to quickly go search the tomb. Herod then turned his attention back to the prisoner. "Now, let's talk about Phasael."

Once again, King Herod stepped aside. To the delight of General Sosius, Philoneus stepped in and started pounding on the royal prisoner with his big beefy fist...

****

"For the sake of peace, I offer forgiveness..."

****

After being wailed upon with several brute punches to his face, Antigonus cried out, "He took his own life!" He spat out a mouthful of blood.

"To escape your torture, no doubt!" King Herod snarled as Philoneus prepared to backhand him.

"I tried to save him!"

Herod gestured for Philoneus to hold. "Save him! So you could torture him to find out my whereabouts!! That is why my brother took his life!!"

"He was protecting you?" Antigonus murmured. With a smirk, he cackled, "And I thought he was just a coward."

His words were met by a sharp crack on the jaw by King Herod's fist. Just as the king prepared to punch him again, upon receiving a sack from one of his men, Sohemus interrupted and showed it to Herod. "My king...we have it." King Herod released the prisoner and watched as Sohemus approached him with the sack. Taking a moment to prepare himself, he slowly opened it. Inside was the mummified head of his brother, Seth. "They found it nailed to the wall," Sohemus said quietly.

"See...I was telling the truth," Antigonus mumbled. "I had it mummified so I could look upon his face and remember my enemy." He looked up at Herod and sneered, "But it was your head I wanted to nail to wall of the throne room."

Enraged, King Herod shoved the sack back into Sohemus' hand and began to pound on Antigonus mercilessly. He suddenly stopped, and glancing at the others, growled, "Leave us!" After they left them alone, Herod bent down and snarled, "You want to hear truth? Then let me enlighten you." He leaned in and quietly whispered something in his ear.

Outraged, Antigonus tried to lunge at Herod, screaming, "MURDERER!!"

The king moved back and scowled, "Now you know my pain."

As Herod stood up, Antigonus snarled, "The people will never call you king!"

Glaring down at him, Herod smiled coldly and replied, "Yes, they will. Once they realize, you will never return."

As Herod walked off, Antigonus called after him, "I will plead my case in Rome!! When they hear what you have done...we shall see who will be king!"

Herod stopped, and pulling out a sealed letter from his garment, he showed it to him and remarked, "Rome? Who said you're going to Rome?" He handed the letter to General Sosius. "Give this to Mark Antony with my compliments." He then looked at Philoneus and ordered, "Make sure he *arrives in one piece."* The burly brute took the dagger out of the flames and came back to the prisoner. *Antigonus' screams echoed throughout the prison as the king walked out, leaving the Roman general to watch.*

****

Raising his hand to quiet the crowd, and shouting over the protestors, King Herod announced, "Rest assured. I will take no revenge on my enemies…"

****

In Antioch, Mark Antony shifted his eyes from the letter Herod had sent him, to a large chest of gold, which a servant placed on the table before him. He then shifted his gaze to Antigonus, kneeling on the ground near the entrance of the tent, burned, bloodied and beaten; one of his eyes was swollen shut. Mark Antony looked at the guard standing over him and nodded. The guard drew his sword. "Wait! I am a prince of Judea! I demand to be taken to Rome!" As the sword was raised over his head, finding no mercy in Antony's eyes, Antigonus lowered his head and closing his eyes, uttered, "Curse you Herod!" The guard beheaded him.

****

Herod looked back at his family seated behind him. He turned his gaze to Prince Aris and with a smile, extended his hand. The young prince stepped forward. "This day I make a promise...our beloved prince shall always have a seat at my table, and when he has come of age, I shall name him...High Priest of Judea! I shall love him as my own son, and protect him with my life!" His statement pleased the people; they roared with cheers. Calming them, Herod shouted, "Now begins...the Herodian Dynasty!!"

Trumpets sounding and drums beating, the crowd erupted in cheers: some shouting, "HEROD!" others shouting, "Aris! Aris! Aris!"

36

I WILL HAVE YOUR HEAD

[35 BC...]

Almost 40, King Herod raised his golden cup. His mother, brother and sister Salome, along with Queen Miriam and Princess Alexandra were seated at the head table in the opulent banquet hall of Prince Aris' palace in Jericho.

Being King of Judea for almost 3 years, Herod looked around at all the guests gathered in the large hall and announced, "On this truly grand occasion, we gather to celebrate two great events! The birth of my son—Prince Alexander!!" The crowd cheered as Miriam stood up and showed them the young prince, barely a month old. Cypros was holding her granddaughter, Salampsio—now almost two. "And a one year celebration of Jerusalem's youngest High Priest..." King Herod continued, "We honor, Prince Aris!"

Ecstatic cheers filled the room as the crowd chanted, "ARIS! ARIS! ARIS!!" His mother looked to his seat, troubled to see it empty. Suddenly, the doors of the banquet hall flung open. The cheers quickly died down as Ophellius walked in, drenched in water. His wet footsteps squelching across the marble floor, came to a halt in the center of the room. He was carrying a boy, a teenager, dripping with water, his arms and legs flopping around lifelessly.

Ophellius laid the boy down on the floor, and looking up at Princess Alexandra, said sombrely, "I found him face down in the pool."

For a brief surreal moment, Alexandra wondered why he was looking at her, but as she looked at the boy's face, she dropped her cup. She stood there hyperventilating and shaking her head while Queen Miriam screamed his name. Sofera took her infant from her hands as Miriam ran over to the boy. Falling to her knees, she began to sob, "Aris! ARIS!!"

As a crowd began to gather, Princess Alexandra slowly pushed her way through them. Her hands cupped over her mouth, tears streaming down her face, she pushed others out of the way as she fell to her knees in the puddle of water surrounding the lad. She looked at the lifeless body of her son; the only words passing from her lips were, "No, no, no, no, NO, NO!!!" Her words became a scream as she touched her son's face. His skin was cold and clammy. Trembling, Alexandra cradled the boy in her arms: her agonizing screams echoing throughout the palace.

The bejeweled gold crown resting on his head, his steely eyes devoid of emotion, King Herod stared numbly at the lifeless Prince while the room erupted into chaos.

Amidst screams and wails, priests tearing their robes in grief, and guards trying to calm the guests, a voice rang out, "HEROD!!" The crowd parted, leaving a clear line of sight as Alexandra looked up at him and pointing, screamed, "YOU DID THIS!! MURDERER!! YOU KILLED MY SON!!!" She laid the boy down and got up. Snatching a knife from off a nearby table, she started marching towards Herod, determined to stab him.

Zoltan—who Herod had promoted to Captain of the Royal Guards—caught her, and wrestling the weapon from her hand, dragged her back. Hysterical, she railed, "He was just 17 and you killed him! I know it was you, Herod! I know it was you!! As God is my witness! I will have your head! You hear me, Herod!! I WILL HAVE YOUR HEAD!!" Her voice trailing off down the hallway, all heads (including Miriam's) turned in silence and stared at King Herod.

[To be continued...]

The SAVIOR journey continues with the next exciting installment entitled...

SAVIOR
BOOK II

TYRANT

AMYZONN KNIGHT

For details on this and other installments or additions in the Savior Book Series; as well as other Heroic Books, projects and merchandise, please visit...

EPIC ENTERTAINMENT TIMLESS FAITH

www.HeroicEntertainment.com

or contact us at **info@heroicentertainment.com**

SAVIOR
BOOK SERIES

Amyzonn Knight

BOOK I

KING HEROD

BOOK II

TYRANT

BOOK III

VENGEANCE

BOOK IV

THE TYRANT, THE DEVIL AND THE KING OF KING

BOOK V

FALLEN ANGEL | RISEN KING

For Information on changes or additions to this Book series, please visit www.HeroicEntertainment.com.

AKNOWLEDGEMENTS

Special Thanks To

Shekhinah Byfield

Bev Byfield

Sherryann Boyce

Sonia Brown

Priscilla Lawrence

Yuliya Yanishevska

The incredibly talented Heroic Cast and Crew who helped bring this project to life

&

Family and friends for their support